Drama High: Street Soldiers

L. Divine

Dedication

To Trayvon Martin. May your soul rest in power.

Praise for *Drama High*

"...Attributes the success of Drama High to its fast pace and to the commercial appeal of the series' strong-willed heroine, Jayd Jackson."
—*Publisher's Weekly* on the DRAMA HIGH *series*

"Abundant, Juicy drama."
—*Kirkus Reviews* on DRAMA HIGH: HOLIDAZE

"The teen drama is center-court Compton, with enough plots and sub-plots to fill a few episodes of any reality show."
—*Ebony* magazine on DRAMA HIGH: COURTIN' JAYD

"You'll definitely feel for Jayd Jackson, the bold sixteen-year-old Compton, California, junior at the center of keep-it-real Drama High stories."
—*Essence* Magazine on DRAMA HIGH: JAYD'S LEG-ACY

"Our teens love urban fiction, including L. Divine's Drama High series."
—*School Library Journal* on the DRAMA HIGH *series*

"This book will have you intrigued, and will keep you turning the pages. L. Divine does it again and keeps you wanting to read more and more."
—*Written* Magazine on DRAMA HIGH: COURTIN' JAYD

"Edged with comedy...a provoking street-savvy plot line, Compton native and Drama High author L. Divine writes a fascinating story capturing the voice of young black America."
—*The Cincinnati Herald* on the DRAMA HIGH *series*

"Young love, non-stop drama and a taste of the supernatural, it is sure to please."
—*THE RAWSISTAZ REVIEWERS* on DRAMA HIGH: THE FIGHT

"Through a healthy mix of book smarts, life experiences, and down-to-earth flavor, L. Divine has crafted a well-nuanced coming of age tale for African-American youth."
—*The Atlanta Voice* on DRAMA HIGH: THE FIGHT

"If you grew up on a steady diet of saccharine-*Sweet Valley* novels and think there aren't enough books specifically for African American teens, you're in luck."
—*Prince George's Sentinel* on DRAMA HIGH: THE FIGHT

Other titles in the *Drama High* Series

THE FIGHT
SECOND CHANCE
JAYD'S LEGACY
FRENEMIES
LADY J
COURTIN' JAYD
HUSTLIN'
KEEP IT MOVIN'
HOLIDAZE
CULTURE CLASH
COLD AS ICE
PUSHIN'
THE MELTDOWN
SO, SO HOOD

~

When I first started writing Drama High it was all about Jayd, her crew, and how I could get their stories out to you. It was also about me, my students, and the drama that seems to carry over from one generation to the next. I love *Drama High,* probably more than I love any of my other projects (yes, I do write other stuff). And because of my affinity for Jayd's drama, I will always be emotionally attached to this series.

When life goes awry I want to curl up in my bed, pull the covers over my head and drown out the rest of the world. But I can't—at least not for too long. Not only because my children need to eat, but also because my readers get hungry, too. Borrowing from the wise words of the late Steve Jobs, I stay hungry and just foolish enough to keep on writing. I do it because of the sheer joy it brings me to know that my readers are feeling my words. I do it because as I've said many times before, as long as you keep reading I will keep writing. I won't stop until the forty-fourth volume of *Drama High* is published.

In order to keep the series moving, you—the readers—must continue to voice your desires and support Jayd's drama. This is the *Harry Potter* of the streets. This is the *Gossip Girls* of the hood. This is your *Drama High.*

Acknowledgements

Thank you to my parents, Dorothy Haskin and Claiborne Logan, who have supported me and my children through this year-plus of not publishing. It's been rough, but my mama and daddy have seen us through with their undying emotional, spiritual and financial support. I know it's sometimes exhausting having an artist as a daughter, but you both keep the prayers coming and I am so grateful that God listens to your words.

A very special thank you to Mama Ingrid and Mrs. Fatimah for being a part of our village. And to my colleague, R. M. Johnson for giving me the push I needed to continue doing what I love. Thank you for your wise and timely inspiration.

THE CREW

Jayd

The voice of the series, Jayd Jackson is a sassy seventeen year old high school senior from Compton, California who comes from a long line of Louisiana conjure women. The only girl in her lineage born with brown eyes and a caul, her grandmother appropriately named her "Jayd", which is also the name her grandmother took on in her days as a Voodoo queen in New Orleans. She lived with her grandparents, four uncles and her cousin, Jay and visited her mother on the weekends until her junior year, when she moved in with her mother permanently. Jayd's in all AP classes at South Bay High—a.k.a. Drama High—as well as the president and founder of the African Student Union, an active member of the Drama Club, and she's also on the Speech and Debate team. Jayd has a tense relationship with her father, who she sees occasionally, and has never-ending drama in her life whether at school or at home.

Mama/Lynn Mae Williams

When Jayd gets in over her head, her grandmother, Mama, is always there to help. A full-time conjure woman with a long list of both clients and haters, Mama also serves as Jayd's teacher, confidante and protector. With magical green eyes as well as many other tricks up her sleeve, Mama helps Jayd through the seemingly never-ending drama of teenage life.

Mom/Lynn Marie Williams

This sassy thirty-something year old would never be mistaken for a mother of a teenager. But Jayd's mom is definitely all that. And with her fierce green eyes, she keeps the men guessing. Able to talk to Jayd telepathically, Lynn Marie is always there when Jayd needs her, even when they're miles apart.

Esmeralda

Mama's nemesis and Jayd's nightmare, this next-door neighbor is anything but friendly. Esmeralda relocated to Compton from Louisiana around the same time Mama did and has been a thorn in Mama's side ever since. She continuously causes trouble for Mama and Jayd, interfering with Jayd's school life through Misty, Mrs. Bennett and Jeremy's mom. Esmeralda has cold blue eyes with powers of their own, although not nearly as powerful as Mama's.

Misty

The original phrase "frenemies" was coined for this former best friend of Jayd's. Misty has made it her mission to sabotage Jayd any way she can. Now living with Esmeralda, she has the unique advantage of being an original hater from the neighborhood and at school. As a godchild of Mama's nemesis, Misty's own mystical powers have been growing stronger, causing more problems for Jayd.

Emilio

Since transferring from Venezuela, Emilio's been on Jayd's last nerve. Now a chosen godson of Esmeralda's and her new spiritual partner, Hector, Emilio has teamed up with Misty and aims to make life very difficult for Jayd.

Rah

Rah is Jayd's first love from junior high school who has come back into her life when a mutual friend, Nigel, transfers from Rah's high school (Westingle) to South Bay High. He knows everything about Jayd and has always been her spiritual confidante. Rah lives in Los Angeles but grew up with his grandparents in Compton like Jayd. He loves Jayd fiercely but has a girlfriend who refuses to go away (Trish) and a baby-mama (Sandy) that has it out for Jayd. Rah's a hustler by necessity and a music producer by talent. He takes care of his younger brother, Kamal and holds the house down while his dad is locked-up in Atlanta and his mother strips at a local club.

KJ

KJ's the most popular basketball player on campus and also Jayd's ex-boyfriend and Misty's current boyfriend. Ever since he and Jayd broke up because Jayd refused to have sex with him, he's made it his personal mission to annoy her anyway he can.

Nellie

One of Jayd's best friends, Nellie is the prissy-princess of the crew. She used to date Chance, even if it's Nigel she's really feeling. Nellie made history at South Bay High by becoming the first Black Homecoming princess ever and has let the crown literally go to her head. Always one foot in and one foot out of Jayd's crew, Nellie's obsession with being part of the mean girl's crew may end her true friendships for good if she's not careful.

Mickey

Mickey's the gangster girl of Jayd's small crew. She and Nellie are best friends but often at odds with one another, mostly because Nellie secretly wishes she could be more like Mickey. A true hood girl, Mickey loves being from Compton and her on again/off again man, G, is a true gangster, solidifying her love for her hood. She has a daughter, Nickey Shantae, and Jayd's the godmother of this spiritual baby. Mickey's current boyfriend, Nigel has taken on the responsibility of being the baby's father even though Mickey was pregnant with Nickey before they hooked up.

Jeremy

A first for Jayd, Jeremy is her white, half-Jewish on again/off again boyfriend who also happens to be the most popular cat at South Bay High. Rich, tall and extremely handsome, Jeremy's witty personality and good conversation keeps Jayd on her toes and gives Rah a run for his money—literally.

G/Mickey's Man

Rarely using his birth name, Mickey's original boyfriend is a troublemaker and hot on Mickey's trail. Always in and out of jail, Mickey's man is notorious in their hood for being a cold-hearted gangster and loves to be in control. He also has a thing for Jayd who can't stand to be anywhere near him.

Nigel

The star-quarterback at South Bay High, Nigel's a friend of Jayd's from junior high school and also Rah's best friend, making Jayd's world even smaller. Nigel's the son of a former NBA player who dumped his ex-girlfriend at Westingle (Tasha) to be with Mickey. Jayd's caught up in the mix as both of their friends, but her loyalty lies with Nigel because she's known him longer and he's always had her back. He knows a little about her spiritual lineage, but not nearly as much as Rah.

Chase (a.k.a. Chance)

The rich, white hip-hop kid of the crew, Chase is Jayd's drama homie and Nellie's ex-boyfriend. The fact that he felt for Jayd when she first arrived at South Bay High creates unwarranted tension between Nellie and Jayd. Chase recently discovered he's adopted, and that his birth mother was half-black—a dream come true for Chase.

Cameron

The new queen of the rich mean girl crew, this chick has it bad for Jeremy and will stop at nothing until Jayd's completely out of the picture. Armed with the money and power to make all of her wishes come true, Cameron has major plans to cause Jayd's senior year to be more difficult than need be. But little does she know that Jayd has a few plans of her own and isn't going away so easily.

Keenan

This young brotha is the epitome of an intelligent, athletic, hardworking black man. A football player on scholarship at UCLA and Jayd's new coffee shop buddy, he's quickly winning Jayd over, much to the disliking of her mother and grandmother. Although she tries to avoid it, Jayd's attraction to Keenan is growing stronger and he doesn't seem to mind at all.

Bryan

The youngest of Mama's children and Jayd's favorite uncle, Bryan is a deejay by night and works at the local grocery store during the day. He's also an acquaintance of both Rah and KJ from playing ball around the neighborhood. Bryan often gives Jayd helpful advice about her problems with boys and hating girls. He always has her back, and out of all of her uncles gives her grandparents the least amount of trouble.

Jay

Jay is more like an older brother to Jayd than her cousin. He lives with Mama and Daddy, but his mother (Mama's youngest daughter, Anne) left him when he was a baby and never returned. Jay doesn't know his father and attended Compton High School before receiving his GED this past school year. He and Jayd often cook together and help Mama around the house.

Jayd's Journal

It all feels like a dream, but I know I'm standing in front of my grandparent's house staring at the gruesome scene. I can still hear Pam's raggedy sandals click-clackin' up the block asking for Mama in her quiet, raspy voice. Mama says we have to dedicate three shrines to Pam and feed them daily for the next forty days. She also says that Pam's soul will not rest until her true murderer is brought to justice, but I don't think that's true. I believe it's Mama's soul that won't rest until we catch whoever—or whatever—committed this heinous act. Granted, Esmeralda most likely put one of her loyal legion members up to it, but her hands are just as dirty as if she held the murder weapon herself. Either way I know it wasn't Mickey's ex no matter what the police think.

I'm no fan of helping Mickey's former man, especially after all the hell's he's caused, but I can't let the wrong person go to prison. I know once the shock of the gruesome murder is numbed a bit Mama will focus on bringing Pam's killer to justice, come hell or high water. I just hope it's sooner rather than later because the cops don't look interested in pursuing any other leads. I'm sure they have their reasons for wanting dude off the street, as do we all. But we have to put the right person away for this, if for no other reason than because Esmeralda's power grows stronger every minute she thinks she's gotten away with murder.

Esmeralda's brood has been very quiet next door since the cops started questioning Mickey's ex about his whereabouts this evening, waiting like the rest of us to see what'll happen next. There's apparently some link between he and Pam that I'm not aware of. More than likely she was his client at one time. I don't know what he sells, but I know it's more than weed—whatever Pam was on the last time I saw her was the highest I've ever seen her. She never looked good, but she looked worse than usual, almost as if she were slowly becoming vacant inside.

Mama could always find the soul behind the addict Pam had become, which is why Mama's taking her death so hard. No doubt Esmeralda knew that and used it to her advantage, adding the personal touch of having Pam slaughtered in our driveway. Earlier, when I was literally running away from Esmeralda's canine beasts for my life, she said she had a gift for the queen—a sacrifice were her exact words. What better way to get Mama's attention than to kill one of her own godchildren? I hope Esmeralda enjoys her victory while it last because as with all things this, too, shall fall apart.

PROLOGUE

The south side of Gunlock is the only street in our neighborhood that bends at the corner on the east side, while the shorter of the two sides stops before the bend. Mama and Netta gave a white, seven-day candle with a small amount of palm oil and a penny on top to each neighbor. The entire block is softened by the soft glow from the dancing flames and silenced by the flashing lights from the squad car.

Pam's only been dead a few hours and already the police are convinced they have the only suspect in custody. What happened to in-depth investigations like on *Law and Order*? Where's the forensics team, or at least a cop with a fingerprint duster—something? What happened to innocent until proven guilty?

"Sir, I'm going to need you to put your hands above your head and assume the position," the black officer says.

Mickey's ex looks truly shocked that he's being arrested for this crime. I wouldn't call him innocent, but he certainly didn't slice Pam up.

"For what? I didn't do shit," Mickey's ex says, but the cops aren't buying it.

Our neighbors look on in horror not sure who to believe. Mickey's ex man has been terrorizing the city for as long as he's been walking, so I doubt too many will shed a tear if he goes away for a long, long time—me included. I've been trying to reach Mickey but she's not responding to any of my calls or text messages. I'm sure she'll find out through the hood grapevine soon enough.

"Sir, I'm not going to ask you again." The white officer smiles at one of our most notorious gangster's protest like he's seen this a million times before. "Place your hands on top of your head, turn around and lie flat on the hood of your vehicle."

This time the officer places his right hand on his weapon ready to draw if necessary. The black officer looks at his partner nervously and then at Mickey's man who hasn't moved a muscle.

"Young brother, please do what the officer asks. There's been enough blood shed this evening," Daddy says, stepping off the curb and toward the disturbing scene.

Mickey's ex glares hard at Daddy then back at the officers. I feel like I'm on an episode of *Southland.*

Mama looks at her husband and then back at the officers as tears well up in her tired eyes. Netta places her left hand on Mama's shoulder for support.

"Sir, I'm going to have to ask you step back," the white officer says, putting his hands out and stopping Daddy's advance. "Please don't interfere with official police business."

Daddy stops in his tracks and looks at our neighbors stand quiet against this injustice. He shakes his head from side to side, completely exasperated.

"But I didn't do it," Mickey's former man repeats for the umpteenth time but the police officers couldn't care less. As far as they're concerned, this young, black male with a record is in the right place at the right time. Usually I wouldn't give a damn about helping Mickey's ex, but this isn't his style. He's more of a shoot 'em-up-and-keep-driving kind of gangster. Shanking somebody isn't his usual mode of operation and we all know it.

"Do you have just cause to arrest this young man for the crime you've accused him of?" Daddy asks the officers who look irritated and terrified at the same time.

"Are you a lawyer, sir?" the younger, black officer asks as he looks at his partner, who tightens the handcuffs on his victim's hands before lifting him by the back of his shirt. I notice Officer Bagley's name on his badge who looks to be about the same age as Daddy. The older officer looks to be in his sixties and close to retirement.

"No, I'm not," Daddy answers, restraining the anger present in his voice. "I'm a pastor."

Mickey's ex looks at Daddy like a scared child and I'm right there with him. But ultimately like the rest of us, Daddy's helpless to stop the law from taking over.

The older officer smiles as the two share a look and roll their eyes in Daddy's direction. I know Daddy wants to put his holiness aside and slap the hell out of them both, but he doesn't let them get the best of him.

The heat in my head begins to rise and I feel a vision coming on. Suddenly, Daddy's in his twenties and this all too familiar scene's now taking place in the past. Before I can get completely caught up in the rapture, the officers slam the car door, locking their unwilling passenger in the back seat.

"Well, Pastor, why don't you pray for this boy's soul and let us take care of the rest."

I wish I could see the older officer's badge. I need a name to refer to this jackass by for future reference.

"How many times I gotta tell y'all pigs I ain't no damn boy," Mickey's ex yells through the cracked window. "I'm a man. A grown ass man."

Daddy again looks like a young man instead of a grandfather. I have a feeling Daddy's been in a similar position before.

"Mama, what are we going to do?" I ask, but my grandmother's too distraught over Pam's death to even think about helping Mickey's former man right now.

Netta pats Mama on the shoulder with one hand and wipes away her tears with the other. I look at them both sadly and wish we could do more.

"We're going to feed the ancestors and Iku to ensure Pam's travels are harmonious during her transition." Mama turns around with Netta beside her.

I follow them toward the backhouse while looking back at Mickey's ex-man struggle in the back of the patrol car. For a moment I swear I can hear him pleading like a little boy for his mother to get him out of this mess—I never even thought of him as having a family before now.

"Mama, what about him?" I ask, gently stopping Mama with my hand on hers, forcing her to acknowledge the common scene of a black man going down for a crime he didn't commit. "We have to help, especially when we know the real murderer's next door."

Netta spits on the ground at the thought of our next-door neighbor and says something in Creole. I don't know the exact translation, but it didn't sound like a blessing. Mama looks across the fenced in back yard and stares intently at Esmeralda's back porch. A couple of hours ago it was alive with light, animals and her loyal followers. Now it's pitch black and completely quiet.

"We are helping him by helping Pam first." Mama steps through the old gate separating the front yard from the back and walks past her loyal dog, Lexi, who wakes up and joins the procession toward the back house.

"But Mama, they're leaving," I say, looking back helplessly. "We have to do something. This isn't right."

The more he resists the more painful it'll be. I wish he'd stop struggling and that Mama would use her coercive vision on the officers to make them hold off, but Mama's not hearing me.

"And what would you have me do, Jayd?" Mama asks from the front of the short line. Netta jumps slightly at the shrill nature of her best friend's voice. Mama's beyond angry: She's mad as hell. "Do you want me to go out there and tell the police how to do their jobs? Then I'd be in the back of the police car, too and that'll never happen to me again. Hell no," Mama says, opening the door to the small house attached to the back of the garage. She looks like she's reliving a memory she's yet to share with me, but I know during her days as an activist she had her fair share of run-ins with the law down south. And apparently, so did my grandfather.

"Then what are we going to do?" I ask, following Mama and Netta inside and closing the door behind me.

Mama turns on the light switch and dims the setting to a softer hue. She directs me to light the seven-day candles on the two window seals in the main room while Netta lights the ones in the kitchen. Mama washes her hands and we follow suit ready to work.

"We're going to do what we do best," Mama says, glancing at the spirit book on the tall, kitchen table in the center of the intimate space. "The true power of persuasion lies in the spirit world and in the streets, not in pleading with officers who don't give a damn." Mama opens the refrigerator door and takes out the buttermilk, a few vegetables and eggs and places them next to the spirit book. "The masses have more power than a so-called justice system can ever embody. We have our work cut out for us, and only forty days and nights to get it done." Mama then removes a freshly plucked chicken and places it inside the sink.

After retrieving the necessary dishes and cooking tools from the cabinets, Netta instinctively inspects the various herb jars lining the counter and I begin sorting the items on the table.

"Sometimes you have to take matters into your own hands, Little Jayd," Netta says, placing the jars of rosemary, lemon balm, sage, and other dried herbs on the table.

"That's when we let go and let God," Mama adds, placing the clean carcass on a cutting board. "We practice the utmost faith in the Creator by having faith in ourselves. We can do this because God has put this situation in front of us. And at the risk of using yet another cliché, God doesn't give us more than we can handle."

"Never, not ever," Netta chimes in between hums of one of my favorite Oshune songs. She has such a pretty voice.

"That said, little Jayd, yes I believe we can make a difference. I know we can do what the police won't," Mama says. "We will find Pam's killer." Mama chops the chicken into pieces with a quickness. I know it's not the bird she's thinking about serving up on a platter: It's Esmeralda's head.

"Never allow the people who let you down keep you down, Jayd," Netta says like she's in church.

"God is the only one who can give and take all things, and that's the only opinion I truly give a damn about," Mama says before leading a quick prayer to the ancestors to bless our work. "There's just as much blood shed in these streets of Compton as there is in New Orleans. Now, those ancestors are calling for justice and it's our duty to answer."

I'm glad to hear that we're doing something about Esmeralda's latest crime. It's time to go H.A.M. on the house next door in a serious way. By the time we're done, they'll never know what hit them.

"Lust takes and love gives."
-Mama
Drama High, volume 3: Jayd's Legacy

Chapter 1
NO LOVE

"Jayd, Jayd. Is your Mama home?"

The sound of sandals quickly flapping wakes me out of my sleep. This feels too real to be a dream. I can hear Pam's shrill voice in the darkness but can't tell where it's coming from.

"Pam, where are you?" I ask. The darkness begins to fade as the sun rises and slits of light bursts through the blinds. I'm sleeping inside Netta's salon. What the hell?

"I'm in the alley. Hurry up, girl! I need to talk to your Mama."

I walk cautiously through the empty shop with my hands out in front of me, my vision still limited by the twilight. I make my way to the wall in the washroom and flick the light switch on illuminating the small space.

"Jayd, where's your Mama?" Pam repeats. "I need to talk to her."

The urgency in Pam's voice frightens me a bit as I make my way onto the porch where I can see Pam standing on the other side of the screen door.

"What's the matter?" I ask. Something tells me not to let her in but I have to. Mama always told me to take care of Pam, even when she's at her worst.

"They trying to get me, Jayd," Pam says, looking around the vacant alley like someone's hot on her trail. She's dressed in a dark hoody and sweats—far from her usual streetwalker attire.

"Who, Pam? The police?" This wouldn't be the first time she's been on the run for one thing or another. I notice her stomach's heavily protruded. Whether Pam knows it or not, she's about to be a mother—again—if this baby makes it. We're still not clear about what happened to the last one she had.

"No. Them," Pam says, pointing toward the opening at the south end of the alley that leads out to Greenleaf Boulevard.

I open the screen door and follow her eyes. It's Rousseau and his canine gang slowly making their way in our direction.

"Pam, get inside!" I scream, trying to force Pam through the backdoor, but her ice-cold skin shocks me and I let go.

"Jayd, get your Mama! She's the only one who can help me now."

"Pam, I don't know where Mama is," I say, realizing that I'm alone in the shop for the first time. Something's definitely up if Netta and Mama left me here by myself. "You can wait for her inside. Evil can't step foot over our thresholds."

Netta's shop—like the spirit room—is under Mama's spiritual protection with a shrine for Legba posted at each entrance. He's the orisha over the crossroads and guards his children fiercely.

"I can't come in, not without an invitation from the queen herself." Pam lifts her hood revealing pitch black eyes and ashen gray skin.

I jump back and instinctively avoid looking directly at the horrific sight. What the hell is wrong with Pam? I don't really know how these things work, but maybe she's having a bad reaction to whatever drugs she's on.

"Pam, stop tripping and get in here. I can't help you if you don't," I say, watching the deadly army approach, but Pam refuses to listen.

"I can't, Jayd. Tell your Mama I need her." Pam's eyes return to their normal brown color as she starts to walk away from Rousseau's brood and the shop. "Promise me you'll give her the message."

"I promise, Pam. Pam, wait!" I scream after her but it's no use.

Pam disappears into the adjacent parking lot belonging to the gas station next door. Rousseau and his crew follow after her ignoring me altogether. I relock the screen and step back inside the shop locking the backdoor behind me.

"Jayd, wake up before you're late to school," Bryan says, peaking his head through Mama's bedroom door, who's nowhere to be found just like in my dream.

I have to tell Mama about Pam's message from beyond the grave. I know that shit was too real to be a simple dream.

"Okay, I'm up." I throw the covers back and let the cool air finish waking me. It's been a while since I slept in my old bed and it felt good. The couch at my mom's house is okay, but there's nothing like a mattress to solidify a good night's sleep.

I glance at the clock on the DVD player and wonder where Mama could be at six in the morning. Then it all comes flashing back to me: Esmeralda's youthful transformation, Rousseau's dogs chasing me, and Pam's murder. Maybe Mama and Netta got an early start on the day's spirit work—God knows there's always enough to go around.

It's funny how the world seems to stand still early in the morning. Even the birds are quietly collecting their breakfast of unsuspecting worms and dew to drink. The neighborhood mutts are rummaging through trashcans left out for the weekly collection. Mr. Gatlin, our mean ass-neighbor across the street, collects his newspaper and ignores me, as usual. He and I are the only two people outside.

It was too late for me to drive back to Inglewood and expect to get any kind of sleep before school this morning. Mama and Netta both insisted that I stay the night and I didn't object. Besides, it was nice sharing a room with my grandmother again. My uncle Bryan didn't even give me any flack this morning for interrupting his daily routine, which he now starts a few minutes earlier due to my absence. I think he missed our morning chats as much as I did.

I haven't left for school from my grandparents' house since last year and haven't missed the lack of privacy or bathroom space in the small house. Bryan's ass is still funky and so is everyone else's. Mama and Netta talked until I fell asleep about what the plan of action will be to organize the neighbors. Between Daddy's congregation and Mama's loyal clientele, they'll be able to call to duty over two hundred people to seek justice for Pam and by default, Mickey's former man.

Mama and Netta were probably out before sunrise making and posting signs all over the neighborhood with Pam's pictures on them—both before and after crack hit her like a freight train. Mama, Daddy and others will hit the streets posting more signs, knocking on doors and talking to people. Daddy's already reactivated the Neighborhood Watch, calling the local police department out for not being more active in our community. Mama and Netta have designated the beauty shop as ground zero for the operation's creative needs while they'll hold meetings at Daddy's church.

I never knew how good my grandparents could be in a crisis situation. They're both excellent community organizers. I guess that's why they fell in love so quickly back in the 1970's. They were young, impetuous and passionate about their individual causes. Right now, nothing else matters except for getting justice for Pam because no one else really cares. The media rarely reports on missing persons in our hood unless there's a salacious murder of someone other than a crackhead to go along with it. They're still the same strained couple behind closed doors, but as far as our small city of Compton is concerned Pastor and Mrs. James are a force to be reckoned with.

I step down the front porch steps toward my mom's *Mazda Protégé* and silently unlock the doors via the remote keychain. When I open the passenger's side door to set my backpack and purse down, Mr. Gatlin frowns at me from his front yard across the street—the feeling is mutual. I shut the car door and walk around to the other side ready to roll. After we exchange a tense look, he turns his attention toward his ex-girlfriend's yard. Mr. Gatlin stares forlornly at our neighbor, Esmeralda's house where her new beau, Rousseau exits the black front porch gate with a bucket and rubber gloves like he's about to wash the car they don't have.

"Bonjour, mi amor," Rousseau says, slamming the iron gate behind him.

I can't see his eyes through his dark sunshades but I can still feel his piercing stare. There should be some sort of law against harassing your neighbors no matter how subtle the attack. Even Mr. Gatlin disappears into his home at the sight of his replacement.

"I'm not your love, no matter what language you say it in." I'm tired of Rousseau's strange ass and his canine crew. If I don't get out of here soon I'm going to be late for school and I still need to grab a muffin and some juice from the student store. There's only cereal and no milk for breakfast—typical.

"Oh, mi petite," Rousseau says. "Why so rude? You did not rest well last night, I assume?"

Assume my ass. If he's anything like his woman he knows exactly why I can't stand his ass. I attempt to ignore Rousseau but his gaze is too strong, much like Esmeralda's.

"Esmeralda needs to keep her pets on a tighter leash before they get hurt," I say, staring back. I'm over being afraid to look folks in the eye. My ancestors are too powerful for that shit.

"What is that supposed to mean?" he asks, tossing the dirty water from the bucket out onto their front lawn.

"It means I've got something for your ass if you don't get off of mine." Rousseau tried to get to me last night through his dogs. If there's a next time, I'm not running. The spirit book has to have something to deal with his kind once and for all.

"Sounds intriguing, young queen." Rousseau smiles, displaying his yellow fangs. "I anxiously await the opportunity to see what exactly it is you'd like to share with me."

"Is everything okay, Jayd?" Mama asks as she and Netta pull up in front of the house causing Rousseau to retreat back inside their creepy menagerie.

I often wonder where Misty and her mom sleep. I've been in Esmeralda's house on a few unfortunate occasions and it's smaller than ours with a literal zoo inside.

"Yeah, just rushing off to school. I don't want to start the week off late." I want to tell Mama all about my morning but it's not the right time. "I love you, Mama. I'll call you later."

"You need to come back here after school, Jayd. We'll need all the help we can get at the county jail. I also want to keep a close eye on you until we figure this out," Mama says, glancing next door. I understand the urgency in her voice, but my gas stank is on empty and my pockets are hurting.

"But Mama, I missed all of my clients in Inglewood this weekend and I have homework to do."

My grandmother looks from her best friend to me, completely unmoved by my pleading.

"I'll see you this afternoon, Jayd," Mama says.

Netta shrugs her shoulders in sympathy but she knows as well as I do that ultimately it's Lynn Mae's show. Well, damn. I guess that's that. My stomach's growling too loudly to continue stating my case. I guess I'll see her back here after school.

I haven't spoken to any of my friends—Keenan included—since our individually dramatic weekends. I know Mickey's still beside herself about Nigel leaving her and Nickey at Rah's house after he found out she was still in contact with her ex, but what can I say? I told her it wasn't a good idea to accept gifts from him, even it was a generous act. Nigel's right: Mickey should feel the repercussions of her actions for once in her life. Maybe she'll learn her lesson this time around.

I also haven't heard from Jeremy since our last date ended on a sour note. I know he thinks that I'm over-reacting but he needs to chill on drinking and smoking every chance he gets. It's not sexy at all and I worry about his safety. I feel guilty for kissing Keenan, but honestly he's becoming the more attractive of the two. Keenan doesn't drink and rarely smokes weed. And, as far as I know, there's no crazy white girl looking to become his wife within the next year.

"What's up, chica?" Maggie asks as we make our way out of the busy main hall. "It feels like I haven't seen you in forever."

We stop and quickly hug before continuing our trek to first period. Now that I have Mrs. Bennett first thing in the morning there's no being late—ever. She'll never get the satisfaction of sending me to detention if I can help it.

"What's up, mami?" Maggie asks as we resume our stride. "How are things?"

"Girl, dramatic as always," I say, shaking my head at the thought of Pam's bloody body in the driveway. "But I don't want to talk about that. How are you doing? Where's your boy?"

"Girl, let me tell you," Maggie says, in her thick, Spanish accent. "Papi and I are just fine, but all couples have their drama. Speaking in which, I heard about you and Jeremy and that puta, Cameron. I got something for that ass if you want, chica. You know you're my girl," Maggie says, looping her left arm through mine, making me smile.

"Nah, I'm good," I say, grateful for the backup. "Cameron's just a distraction. Unfortunately, we've got bigger issues to deal with." I hope Jeremy heeds my advice and chills. I don't care what he says, his daily consumption habits can't be good for anyone to maintain.

"I feel you, girl," Maggie says, waving to her boyfriend, Mario and the rest of their Latino crew, El Barrio. Her little brother, Juan joined South Bay High this year and she's very protective of him. Juan's a cutie, just like Maggie. "I don't want mi hermanito getting twisted with these brujas up here, especially witches like her," Maggie says, pointing across the courtyard to Misty who's walking to class with Emilio.

I wonder how KJ feels about her newfound BFF?

"Maggie, Juan's a freshman. I'm sure he's trying to stay in his lane and date girls his own age," I say, laughing at Maggie's reaction to Misty's latest outfit.

High heels and mini skirts have become a large part of Misty's senior year trademark look, along with her short haircut and blue contact lenses, courtesy of her godmother. Misty looks like a completely different person, and under Esmeralda's, influence that's exactly what she's become.

"I don't know, mija. Misty seems to have a thing for Chicano blood lately. Maybe she's finally reclaiming her other half," Maggie says, referring to Misty's Puerto Rican ancestry on her mother's side.

They rarely claim their roots, with Misty's mother passing for white unless she's in Compton, and Misty only acknowledging her black side no matter where she is. Maggie's right: Misty and Emilio have been nearly inseparable lately. I know that they were initiated together on the same night of my own spiritual right of passage, but I had no idea it would affect Misty like it has.

"Uh oh, "Maggie says, acknowledging KJ and friends entering the crowded yard.

We all need to get a move on before the warning bell rings. I personally prefer to be seated in my first period class before the final bell, leaving me a few moments to mentally prepare for the wrath of Mrs. Bennett. But I don't want to miss this confrontation, either.

"Misty, what the hell are you doing with this bitch-ass fool?" KJ asks, taking Misty by the arm like a pimp mad at his main chick.

"KJ, I'm warning you. Let go," Misty says, glaring at her boyfriend.

This little scene between Misty and KJ is surprising to all of us, mostly KJ. He's used to having Misty under his thumb and her loving it, but not anymore. Misty's transformation from being the cute, around the way girl with a bit of Latin flavor to the dark, near-Goth chick she's become is proving to be a bit much for the most popular basketball player at South Bay High. I only dated KJ briefly, but I never thought he was capable of physical abuse.

"What the hell's going on over there?" Mickey asks, walking over to Maggie and I with Nellie by her side.

I want to ask Mickey if she got my messages last night about her ex being arrested for murder, but I already know that she did. I'll drill her about why she's avoiding the topic later.

I notice Nigel and Chase enter the campus through the parking gate barely on time, as usual. Nigel's temporarily staying with Chase and they're becoming more like brothers every day. Mickey glances in Nigel's direction hoping for some sort of acknowledgement he's softening from their argument at her and Nellie's birthday celebration this past weekend, but it doesn't look like he's in a very forgiving mood.

"KJ's having a moment," Maggie says. "Hasta luego, chica. And don't forget I need my braids hooked up. Mario loves it when I wear my hair like yours," Maggie says, touching my cornrows.

"I got you." I hug Maggie and decide it's time for me to get to class as well, even if I don't want to miss the drama. Lucky for me there's always more right around the corner.

"Or else what, Misty?" KJ says, tightening his grip. "Your little boy toy here's going to kick my ass?" KJ says, causing his main homie, Money and a newcomer to their athletic clique, Brandon to laugh.

"I don't need Emilio to fight my battles for me, although he can," Misty says, placing her free hand on her hip while popping her gum.

Oh, no she didn't. KJ looks like he's about to blow a gasket he's so pissed. It's one thing to flirt with another dude in front of your man, but to shame him in the presence of the other dude and a crowd is crossing the line.

"Misty, if you don't stop hanging out with this square ass punk we're over." KJ tightens his grip on Misty who smiles wickedly at her man.

I don't know if the spell Misty put on KJ last year after he broke up with me and his ex crazy side chick, Trecee, is taking a turn for the worse, or if making him have a Chris Brown moment was all a part of the plan, but this isn't a good look. Not that I care all that much about my ex, but it's our senior year and KJ can't afford any blemishes to his otherwise pristine school record. College recruiters look at the total package and he needs his to stay in tact if he wants a full ride.

"Damn, she looks like she's about to get her ass beat," Nellie says, as other students begin to clear out in an effort to beat the late bell.

I'm torn between intervening in what I know is none of my business and dealing with Mrs. Bennett's mouth if I'm late.

"Good," Mickey says, unsympathetically. "Some bitches need a good beat down to act right." Mickey looks pleased at the demise of Misty's relationship. We're all surprised it lasted this long, but I don't want anyone to get hurt over the shit.

"Y'all are so wrong," I say, shocked at my girls' lack of compassion for another female. I don't care what Misty's done, there's never a good excuse for a man to put his hands on a woman.

"And so are you, always trying to save stray dogs. You need to let a bitch be, Jayd. Misty brought this on herself." Mickey's right—sort of—but I can't stand here and watch this insanity continue.

"KJ, let go of her arm," I say, walking over to the scene of the near-crime. Emilio and Misty look pleased at my intervention. I hope I didn't just walk into one of their evil traps.

"Mind your business, Jayd," KJ says, not taking his eyes or hand off of his girlfriend. "This doesn't concern you."

Money and Brandon stand on the sidelines, as usual, watching their boy dig a whole for himself. What kind of friends are they?

"I don't need your help, Osunlade. But thanks for your concern," Misty says, slurring my spirit name. How does she even know it? Mama, Netta, my mom and Mr. Adewale were the only ones present when it was given to me. "I've got just as much power as you do now, or don't you remember?" Misty smiles, revealing her shiny, sharp incisors for my personal view even though there are others around.

How is it that I'm the only one who notices Emilio and Misty are the latest shape-shifting couple at South Bay High?

"This is your doing, isn't it, Jayd?" KJ asks, finally releasing Misty's arm and turning his heat toward me. "What, did you put some sort of voodoo curse on Misty to make me break up with her because you want me back?"

"As if, fool," I say, disgusted by KJ's accusation on so many levels. "I don't need to cast spells on dudes to make them like me. You need to take a closer look at the latest vampire you've been laid up with."

Misty and Emilio exchange a knowing look, satisfied at this morning's events.

"Jayd, whatever," Money says, butting in just to hear himself talk. "We all know you still got it bad for our boy."

Usually Del adds the last two cents for comic relief, but he hasn't been hanging with his boys so far this year. Dudes have fallouts just like us girls: Drama's an equal opportunity employer.

"Yeah, okay. I've got to get to English and read some real fiction, not the unnecessary bull y'all have going on here," I say, taking off to class.

The late bell begins to ring as soon as I start my sprint toward the Language Hall across the courtyard. Lucky for me the classroom door is open. I make it to my seat completely out of breath but before the bell stops ringing, much to Mrs. Bennett's displeasure.

"Thank you for joining us this morning, Miss Jackson," Mrs. Bennett says, closing her roll book. "Your morning expository assignments are on the board. Please be prepared to share your essays from last night's homework."

If she weren't so evil, I'd actually enjoy this class. It's not as free-thinking as my junior AP English teacher, Mrs. Malone's class was, but the literature is just as interesting if not more. Mrs. Bennett's a smart lady, no doubt. I had her sophomore year and she was just as mean and equally brilliant as she is this year.

When I was a child, Mama and I used to watch the cartoon *Kirikou and the Sorceress* almost every day. In it, the Sorceress was a beautiful, cunning and wealthy woman who seemed like she was made of pure evil. It took a very special newborn to pluck the thorn out of her back, relieving her suffering and as a result, the suffering of everyone around her. Kirikou also revealed he was a grown ass man at the end, making the Sorceress even happier. Maybe that's what Mrs. Bennett needs: a tall, dark and handsome man to ease her pain and mine as well.

My estranged man, Jeremy and his wannabe wifey, Cameron step inside the full room and each hand the teacher excused tardy slips. It must be nice existing in the good graces of the attendance office like Misty, whose mom also works there.

"It's so nice to see the two of you together," Mrs. Bennett says with a wide smile spread across her chalky face. She's a little too involved in student business for my taste, even if she is a friend of Jeremy's mom.

Jeremy looks at me sadly and I feel his pain. On cue, Cameron steps in front of my ex and smiles victoriously at her handiwork. If she only knew how much I despise her existence she'd back the hell off. But like Mickey said, it takes some broads getting completely beat down to learn their lesson. I hope it doesn't come to blows with Cameron, but if it does I'm not holding back. Whether she knows it or not, Cameron's playing with poison and I've had just about all I can take of her madness. Unfortunately, Jeremy's addictions are what got us into this mess and it's going to take a strong antidote to get us out.

"Life is a gamble…Whether or not you play the game is up to you."
-Lynn Marie
Drama High, volume 14: So, So Hood

Chapter 2
NOT GUILTY

Compared to the early morning episode between Misty and KJ the rest of the school day was uneventful. Even Cameron's over-the-top flirting with Jeremy was no match for KJ groveling after an unconcerned Misty during both break and lunch. Mickey and Nellie got a kick out of it, but I was truly disturbed. Whatever Misty's got going on is proving to be both powerful and dangerous. If she can get the school's biggest player to turn in his pimp card, she's definitely got bigger and better things planned for the future.

During break I attempted to divert Mickey's attention long enough to talk about her ex man's arraignment in a few minutes but she wouldn't hear me. And Nellie dominated the lunch conversation talking about her boyfriend, David and their day at church yesterday. Nellie's really on one with this cat but there's something about him I don't trust.

I asked both of my girls if they'd show up to the courthouse for support but they each had something else to do. I can't imagine what since neither of them have jobs nor believe in studying. Mickey's daughter, Nickey Shantae, is at daycare until six and Nellie has nothing to do other than try to fit in where she doesn't belong.

When I pull up to the Compton courthouse members of the Gunlock Block Club are in front of the white building chanting in unison. Mama and Netta made various picket signs and thousands of fliers to pass out to anyone who'll take them. I park at one of the metered spaces up the street ready to lend my support. I'd rather be making money but we all can't have the leisurely choices my girl's apparently do.

"Jayd," one of Mama's more friendly neighbors, Mrs. Gray says to me. She's also one of Daddy's most loyal church members. "Your grandparents are inside. They're about to start the proceedings soon."

Making my way through the lively familiar faces, I step inside the building and stand in line for the security screening. Once through the metal detectors, Mama greets me and leads me to where her, Daddy, Netta and the defendant are awaiting their turn in front of the judge.

"Hey, baby," Mama says, hugging me tightly. She looks more tired than usual. I return the love and take her right hand, falling into step with her quick pace. "The court-appointed attorney has just arrived."

Mama opens the door to a waiting area for defendants and their attorneys. Usually family members would be here for extra support, but since Mickey's ex seems to be missing his we're here to stand in their place. Other than us, the attorney and a police officer are present in the small cubical. There are about twenty identical makeshift spaces in the open area, all filled with other prisoners and their associates.

Mickey's ex smiles when I enter the space. I hate the way he looks at me.

"We're here to support this young man," Daddy says, pointing toward Mickey's ex boyfriend who looks as if he couldn't care less that my grandparents and several other neighbors are present to proclaim his innocence. The others more so out of fear than faith, but Mama and Daddy know it wasn't him that did this to Pam. It was our diabolic neighbor, Esmeralda and her manimal who are responsible for this. We don't know how yet, but the truth will be revealed if Mama has anything to say about it. And much to the officer's offense, she's got plenty to share this afternoon.

"There's no way in hell, heaven or the afterlife that this young man committed such a gruesome killing and you know it," Mama vehemently says.

Netta nods her head in agreement.

"I even called one of my clients who works for the local news. She'll be down here soon to report on this injustice." Netta's on fire today. I'm sure this is the last thing the courthouse expected in this case.

"Ma'am, I don't know any such thing. I've been on these streets for twenty-two years and have seen much worse done by more unassuming characters than him," the officer says, pointing at the defendant with disgust.

I can see he's already made up his mind, damn the trial. "You never know someone's a heathen until it's too late."

"I ain't no heathen, fool," Mickey's ex says. Part of his hair's half braided and the rest is sticking straight up—not the best look for an appearance before the judge. He scratches his scalp revealing his shackled wrist. "And I just got out the joint. Why would I waste more time going back in over a crackhead? Shit, I didn't want that strawberry dead. She was one of the best friends a nigga like me could have, if you know what I mean," he says, basically admitting he's a drug dealer without saying the incriminating words verbatim.

"Son, please stop talking. You'll only aggravate the officer," Daddy says. He shifts in the hard, metal seat looking just as stressed out as Mama does.

"So this is your son?" the attorney asks, flipping through his paperwork. "It's taking some time for me to retrieve his entire file. I just got assigned his case a few moments ago."

"Hell nah this old dude ain't my daddy," Mickey's ex says. "My pops died in the struggle."

"What struggle was that?" Mama asks, genuinely interested in this dude's story.

I just want this to be over with as soon as possible so we can all get back to living our lives. For months it's been one thing after another, and I for one am tired of the constant intrusions on my personal time.

"The struggle in the streets. There's a war going on out there in case you haven't noticed. It's hard out here for a pimp." Mickey's ex gets a laugh out of his own ignorance.

Too bad he's the only one present who does. I can see why my girls didn't want to waste time supporting him: he won't even help himself.

"A pimp? Really? That's what you consider yourself?" Mama's question and piercing gaze calm him down, though I'm sure he doesn't know why he's suddenly chilled out.

"Nah. I'm just saying five-o don't make it easy on us. We out here just trying to make money to pay the rent; you know what I'm saying? And punk asses like this Uncle Tom fool right here want to hold us down," Mickey's ex says, pointing at his court-appointed counsel who's not the least bit offended by his client's words. "It's just like that Occupy Wall Street shit, but realer. We occupying these streets and trying to get The Man off our asses—real talk."

"That's the dumbest shit I've heard all day, and it's been a very long day," Mama says, causing the cop to let out a small chuckle. Mama shoots the officer a stern look that lets him know she's not on his side, either.

"It was a great speech," Netta says. "Stupid, but great."

"Man, whatever," Mickey's ex says. He's got one more time to disrespect Mama or Daddy in front of me before I snap.

The attorney looks through more paperwork a court clerk just handed him and quickly sorts through the large file. "According to the court docket we're up next."

"Mr. and Mrs. James, will you be providing outside counsel for the defendant?" the attorney asks. I bet he'll be glad to get off this case if it moves on to trial. He's yet to refer to Mickey's ex by his birth name, which I'm dying to know.

"Yes, I think I will be. Let me make a call," Daddy says, stepping away.

"Excellent," the attorney says, standing up and claiming the file. "I'll be right back to collect the defendant for his arraignment. I assume we're entering a guilty plea and should be out of there in a few minutes."

"You assumed wrong, fool," Mickey's ex says between gritted teeth. "I already told your punk ass I'm innocent."

The attorney looks surprised at his client's intensity. He nods his salt and pepper head in acknowledgment of his clients' plea before leaving. I'm sure Daddy has a favor or two to call in from a few of his congregation members with law practices in the hood. I hope one of them takes this case because this lawyer is definitely the wrong one if we plan on winning.

"What's your name, child?" Mama asks, attempting to lock onto his eyes but he refuses to look directly at my grandmother for too long.

"I'm like the Gladiator; you can just call me Gangster," he says to an unamused Mama.

"You do realize gladiators were slaves, don't you?" Leave it to my grandmother to attempt to educate the chosen ignorant.

"Whatever, old lady," he says to Mama who now looks like she wants to slap the gold teeth out of his mouth. "You can call me G."

"You know what, G?" I say, stepping to the center of the small square and standing directly in front of him. "You need to be grateful my grandparents care enough about your sorry ass to show up when it's obvious no one else does."

Mama and Netta put their hands on my shoulders to calm me down but I've had enough. I know I'm not supposed to cuss in front of my elders but this jackass has gone too far.

"I love it when you talk dirty to me, baby," G says, smiling wickedly.

There's the fool we all love to hate. Before I can fully tear into his ass, the officer gets the signal from the attorney.

"Well, G, you're up next," the smug officer says, taking G by the arm and leading him toward the courtroom. "I'm sure you know the drill." Unfortunately, he knows the way this part of the system works all too well.

"That boy should be a lawyer or detective or something as elusive as he is," Mama says, trying to calm herself down. She looks frustrated, scared and pissed off—all of the common symptoms after an encounter with the gangster kind.

"G's the closest thing to a name I've ever heard him refer to himself by, and I've had the unfortunate pleasure of knowing him for over two years," I say, wrapping my right arm around Mama's shoulders. She looks completely worn out. I'll remind her later to pay Dr. Whitmore a visit as soon as possible.

"Have you visited the good doctor yourself lately?" My grandmother asks, responding to my thought aloud.

"Touché, Mama. Touché'," I say.

Netta smiles at us both as we collect our purses ready to roll.

"Where's that boy's family?" Netta asks, still concerned about public enemy number one. "No one should have to face a murder trial alone."

After a few minutes, Daddy steps back inside the room and waves for us to leave. It's about time. A sistah's got homework to do, and if I can fit in a couple of heads this afternoon I can make my gas money for the week. I'm back to eating *Top Ramen* for the time being until I can stack my cash back up. If Mama let's me get my hustle on, one good weekend should put me back on top.

"That young man's going to need more than his relatives to get him through this," Mama says, leading the way out. "He needs all of God's army on his side as self-destructive as he is."

Daddy ushers us into the hallway and toward the exits where the neighbors have dispersed for the day. "Do you know that boy was inside threatening to kill the real murderer once he finds out who he is?" Daddy says.

"Or she," Mama says, her green eyes aglow.

"With an inevitable war brewing between Esmeralda and that boy there's more evil threatening the neighborhood than we can imagine," Netta says, cryptically. "We need to stop them both before they kill each other and take more innocent lives along the way."

I can only imagine what kind of vengeful plans Esmeralda's camp and G's fellow gang members are concocting as we speak. Both sides are equally dangerous even if G doesn't know what kind of power he's dealing with. When he finds out that Esmeralda's the one behind his latest charge all hell is going to break loose.

"Sometimes we're our own worst enemy," Mama says, stepping outside and taking a deep breath. I spent most of the sunny day inside.

"Yes, indeed," Netta says, eyeing the dozens of people walking in and out of the courthouse.

"When self-loathing becomes toxic, that hatred seeps into the surrounding air choking the life out of every living thing around it. And like all weeds, it must be destroyed so the plant can thrive," Mama says, following her best friend down the steps as Daddy leads the way toward the parked cars. "Where there is fear there can be no love. Where there is life there can be no death. Do you understand, Jayd?"

"Yes, ma'am. I do," I say, kissing my grandparents and godmother good-bye.

Mama's right. Much like the veve charm hanging from the eleke around my neck, there are many roads to choose from. I'm pretty sure the path G's chosen will lead to his ultimate demise if he's not careful.

"You act like your shit don't stink. And trust me, it does."
-Bryan
Drama High, volume 14: So, So Hood

Chapter 3
TOXIC

Mama wanted me to spend the night again last night but I needed some time and space to myself. Lucky for me today is a customary short Tuesday for faculty meetings giving me a much-needed early day out of school. It's also Mama and Netta's day to close the shop and do each other's hair, even if they've requested my presence.

So far, I've managed to avoid engaging in the drama between Cameron and Jeremy all day, focusing instead on how to figure out what Misty and Emilio are up to. KJ was on her ass like white on rice today, but Misty didn't even entertain him—that's anything but normal.

Finally reaching my locker in the middle of the vast hall, I quickly unlock it to switch out my books for tonight's homework. Maybe if I can get to the shop early enough they'll let me go in a couple of hours.

"Jayd, wait up," Nellie says, catching me off guard as she, Reid and Laura—the current president and first lady of the Associated Student Body—walk in through the opposite end of the hall where the entrance to the main office is located. Nellie giggles excitedly about something I know I don't want to hear about, wraps up her conversation and heads my way. So much for me making a clean get away.

"What's up?" I ask, eyeing other students chatting it up.

It's the perfect day for clubs to catch up on recruiting new members, reminding me that I need to call an African Student Union meeting soon. It'll be our first for the year. As president, I should be looking forward to it but I'm not. As with everything else in my life, I'm sure the meeting will bring more drama than necessary.

"Jayd, can you drop me off at the salon? Mickey was supposed to give me a ride but she's nowhere to be found," Nellie says, flipping her long weave over her right shoulder and subsequently dropping her keys.

Nellie bends forward to pick them up and I spot the new growth at the base of her neck. No wonder she's in such a hurry to get to the beauty shop. Her roots are showing her true ancestry and I know Nellie isn't feeling that. She won't even come to one of our ASU meetings let alone go for wearing her hair natural.

"Did you try calling her?" I ask, in no mood to be Nellie's chauffeur. She needs to get a license and a car of her own. Being dependent isn't a good look.

"Of course I did," Nellie says, irritated. "But I think she left campus at lunch. We talked about going after school but I told her I wasn't sure of my plans."

That's a typical Nellie move, always expecting folks to wait around for her. That's also one of the reasons

Chase eventually bounced on her high-maintenance ass.

"Have you ever considered taking the bus?" I ask, charging through the courtyard toward the front parking lot. "If you take the Metro it'll drop you off on Rosecrans, practically right in front of the shop."

"That would take forever," Nellie says to the back of my head. She can keep talking but I have no intentions of diverting my plans for anyone. "Besides, I'm wearing my new *Gucci* boots. They're not made for walking or sitting on a city bus."

"Nellie, I'm on my way to work. Ever heard of it?" I'd offer to do her hair but I know she'd decline, as always. She and Mickey are unimpressed with my skills.

Several seagulls fly above our heads, briefly dimming the bright sunlight. It's a warm, breezy day and the majority of the students leaving campus are on their way to the beach, including Cameron's crew at the other end of the lot. No doubt Jeremy's already in the water. I wish I could chill like them, but as always duty calls for this awkward black girl.

"Jayd, please. I can't miss my appointment. I have bible study tonight and I can't go looking like this," Nellie says, gesturing towards her hair.

Truth be told, Nellie's a beautiful girl. Her mocha complexion and high cheekbones are striking. She doesn't need a weave, heavy make up or expensive clothing to make her standout. Unfortunately, she's the only one who doesn't know how inherently beautiful she really is.

"You look fine, Nellie," I say, trying not to let Cameron's cheery attitude ignite the hater in me. "I'm already running behind schedule as it is."

"I'll give you twenty dollars for gas." Now she's talking my language.

"Okay, Nellie. But don't make this a habit. And for God's sake, girl; learn how to drive."

Nellie rolls her eyes at me but she knows I'm right.

I unlock the car doors and we settle in. It's out of my way but at least it'll give me a chance to really see what's up with Mickey. She's been avoiding me like the plague and I want to know what that's all about. I left her a message last night stating that G pleaded not guilty and wasn't allowed bail because of his recent release from the LA County jail. I don't agree with her still being in contact with her ex, but since she is she should also be there to support him. G seems to have no family, which explains a lot about his behavior. If Mickey's the only friend G's got other than his gang homies, then she needs to be there for him like he's been there for her all of these years.

When we step inside the shop I instantly gag from the chemical fumes sucking all of the oxygen out of the air. In the back of the shop is the nail spa, and in the front is the regular press and curl, barber and braid section. How do these ladies breathe up in here? I'm surprised more of them don't have brain damage or lung disease with the various toxins present in the small space.

One of the stylists is doing a Brazilian Blowout on her client, which Mama says they were doing back in the day when she used to frequent Carnival every year. The straightening method was hazardous then and still is in her opinion. Mickey and Nellie have been coming to CoCo's Cosmetology on Compton Boulevard for years and wouldn't leave for anything in the world, no matter how dangerous the products may be. Affectionately referred to as CoCo's, men and women alike wait for hours to get their hair done here.

"Hey, everyone," Nellie says, waving to the staff and clients alike. "Sorry I'm late. This is my girl, Jayd."

"Hi Nellie and co.," CoCo says, directing us to the waiting area. She's working on tightening a weave and her client looks like she wants to cry.

The shop is bright with fluorescent lights and flat screen televisions on each wall. Everything from the pleather chairs to the hair tools are black, silver or pink. There's even a disco ball hanging from the ceiling causing rainbow rays to bounce off of the mirrors. It feels more like a nightclub than a place of business.

"Is Mickey here?" Nellie asks, claiming a fashion magazine out of one of the baskets on the end table where I notice a braid magazine. It wouldn't hurt for me to see what's new in the business.

"I'm back here getting my nails done," Mickey yells.

Good. I need to look her in the eye when she comes up with an excuse about why she's tripping on her ex after she foolishly put her relationship with Nigel at risk for his ass.

I follow Nellie to the back of the shop where the nail salon is housed. Mickey and three other women are getting the works. It must be nice for my girl to be a teen mom with hood-wifey benefits. Speaking of which, who's bank rolling all of this pampering?

"There she is, Miss M.I.A. herself," I say, posting up against an empty station closest to my girl with my magazine in tow. I hope CoCo doesn't mind if I borrow it; she's got plenty to spare. And it's not the most recent issue so I doubt anyone will miss it.

Mickey rolls her eyes in my direction as Nellie takes a seat in the spa chair next to hers. It must be nice living the ghetto fabulous life without a job. I hope Mickey knows her days are numbered living under Rah's roof with no income. He doesn't play that shit.

"Paula, can I get a mani, pedi and brow wax while I wait for CoCo's chair to clear? Please and thank you," Nellie says, relaxing into the massage chair.

The tall, black woman with blue streaks in her asymmetrically cropped hair nods her head without taking her eyes away from her client's acrylic claws. Nellie places her oversized *Michael Kors* bag on the end table attached to the large chair and slits her eyes at Mickey for leaving her behind. Mickey shrugs her shoulders and refocuses her attention on the large television screen mounted on the wall in front of her. This is the place to hangout even if you're not getting any services.

"So Mickey, did you get my many, many messages about your ex?" I ask, flipping casually through the colorful magazine. I could do all of these styles with the right comb and enough time.

"Yeah, I heard them but I've been busy with Nickey and school. You know how it is," Mickey says, lying through her teeth. Nickey's down for the night by eight and we all know she's never taken any of her schoolwork seriously.

"Mickey, spill it," I say, abruptly closing my magazine. This girl is testing my patience.

Nellie looks at Mickey waiting for the real story, too.

Mickey looks at Nellie and then me, ready to give in. "The reason I can't go to the hearings is because G doesn't want me there."

"Mickey, I don't think that's true," I say. "There was no one there for him at his hearing yesterday except for my family and our neighbors. I know you're probably mad at him over Nigel blowing up, but he needs whatever kind of support he can get."

Nellie looks away pretending to read her magazine. I know there's something they're not telling me.

"Okay, what the hell is going on around here?" I roll the magazine up and place it inside of my purse lest I forget to take it with me when I finally do leave. I know Mama and Netta are watching the clock.

Mickey looks down at her toes soaking in the bubbly water and then back up at me. "We're back together, Jayd," Mickey says. "And G doesn't like his family getting involved in the court system and all that nonsense. By not being there I'm doing exactly what my man wants me to do."

"What the hell is wrong with you, Mickey?" I exclaim, ready to take the rolled up paper out of my purse and smack some sense into my girl. "Have you completely lost your mind, Mickey? If Nigel finds out about this he will never forgive you."

No matter how much she may claim to like this new fool she's seeing, Nellie can't hide her joy about Mickey and Nigel's final demise. The other clients around us listen without intruding, used to witnessing drama in the shop.

"Who gives a shit about how Nigel feels? He didn't care about my feelings when he walked out on me and my daughter." Mickey blows on her freshly painted acrylics completely unconcerned with the foulness of her actions.

"After G sent you those cryptic 'Whore of Babylon' letters the last time he was locked up I thought you understood how unstable dude really is," I say, recalling the fear in Mickey's eyes when she first showed me the red ink-stained pages. I've never seen her so scared of anything, and now she's back in bed with the enemy.

"Girl, he was just mad 'cause me and Nigel were raising Nickey like he and I always planned to do with our kids. And now that Nigel's dropped the ball, I have to do what's right by my family, Jayd."

"Have you talked to Nigel about this? And what about the fact that you're living in his best friends house?"

Nellie looks at me as if to say "Shut the hell up before they end up back together!" but I won't be silenced. My main concern is Nickey Shantae, and Mickey playing house with the notorious felon that killed Nickey's biological father is not in the baby's best interests, damn her hood family dreams.

"You see, that's exactly why I didn't tell your ass a damned thing. I knew you were going to drill me like 5.0." Mickey sucks her teeth but I'm the one who's disgusted.

"Hell yeah you knew I would, Mickey," I say, heated. "This is a hot mess and you know it."

"But it's my hot mess, Jayd. And I'll deal with it the way I see fit."

Mickey's right. I'm tired of playing everybody's mama. I glance at the wall clock and feel Mama calling me from the other side of Compton. If I leave now I can still make it before three.

"I've got to get to work," I say, exasperated with this new information. It was better when I thought Mickey was simply avoiding G. This girl's given me a headache with her ill logic. "See y'all at school tomorrow."

"Thanks for the ride, Jayd," Nellie says, passing me a crisp twenty-dollar bill from her purse. "You should really consider letting CoCo hook you up one day. I think you'd look cute with a fresh cut and some gold streaks in the front."

"Yeah, you'd look like Meghan Good with her short cut," Mickey says, pointing to a picture of the actress in Nellie's magazine. "Sexy for sure."

They're so silly even when we're at odds. My girls mean well but can be a bit much. Mama would kill the barber and me if I ever let anyone other than her, Netta or my mom touch my hair let alone cut it.

"Bye, y'all."

"Holla," Nellie says. She tends to get a little darker once she crosses Central Avenue—Nellie knows her place. She can pretend to be white all she wants in the South Bay, but it ain't too many white folks who can hook a weave up like CoCo can.

The strip mall houses about ten other businesses including a liquor store, beauty supply and clothing boutique. The parking lot is bustling with consumers ready to spend their money. On the way to my car I swear I can hear Pam walking behind me, her sandals just as loud as they were in my dream. I turn around but it's just a stray dog dragging its leash on the ground—too weird. I need to tell Mama about my recent visions as soon as I get to the shop. The last thing I need is another meltdown, and with my head as hot as it is it may only be a matter of time before I go off.

Netta's shop is the complete opposite of CoCo's and so are her clients. Netta mostly services the church crowd, teachers, postal workers and housewives. CoCo's clients are younger, hipper and their employment is never truly disclosed.

"Alafia, Little Jayd," Netta says, buzzing me in. "How is our queen in training doing this afternoon?"

Mama's sitting under one of three blow driers in the front of the shop relaxing while Netta preps the curling and flat irons. The scents of sandalwood and vanilla usher me over the threshold, instantly calming my nerves. The new fragrance for our autumn product line of hair care was my idea. And judging from the peaceful energy in the space, I'd say it was a good blend. Hopefully there's enough of the new hair care batch for me to sample on myself.

"Hi, Mama," I say, bending down to kiss my grandmother who's eyeing me like I'm late, which technically I'm not. "I'm glad to see you two are taking a break from the campaign trail for a moment."

"Yes, my dear, but only for a moment. We have much more to do to get that boy out of jail, no matter how foolish he is."

"He's not the only one," I say, recalling Mickey's relationship revelation. I walk over to Netta's main station, kiss her on the cheek and admire her new cellophane.

Netta's new line of natural hair glass—as she calls it—has been a huge hit. I've been thinking about trying it out myself. Nellie may be right about me needing to switch it up a bit, although I'd never admit that to her. I don't mean a complete transformation like Misty's made, but a little more spunk in my stylo wouldn't be such a bad thing.

"What's that supposed to mean?" Netta asks. "And why do you smell like perm solution and burnt plastic?"

"It means that Mickey has decided to be the ride-or-die chick G wants by his side right now, forget about her and Nigel and their happy hood family. And I smell like this because I dropped Nellie off at CoCo's shop."

Mama acknowledges the strange stench already soaked into my clothes and skin. I replace my *Pink* hoody with my white work apron and reclose the cabinet door. My personal space needs to be cleaned out and probably all of the others do, too. After I wash up I'll get to work on it and the clients' personal beauty boxes. It's been a while since I checked their supply levels.

The yellow curtain separating the front of the shop from the back where the office/shrine room and private bathroom are located is open, allowing a breeze to flow freely through the warm space. I bow to greet the shrine, taking the Florida water from the bamboo mat at its feet and head to the bathroom. Sometimes a quick head cleansing is all I need to get my mojo going.

"That girl's gonna learn her lesson the hard way if she keeps playing with fire," Netta says, smacking hard on her *Big Red* gum. The lavender face soap feels good on my skin washing away all of the oil from my day. This t-zone thing is annoying. Even Mama's daily tea tree and aloe soap can't stop the shine permanently.

"And that boy is pure Shango," Mama says as I reenter the main room ready to work.

She did a spiritual reading on G last night and learned that his head belongs to Shango, the orisha of fire, passion and male virility: a bad combination in a gangster with no guidance. After spending yesterday afternoon with G, Mama's convinced she can save his soul. I hate to doubt my grandmother's skills, but some souls should just be left alone.

"Is he now? That's interesting," Netta says, walking over to her sole client for the day ready to press and curl Mama's shoulder-length locks. She turns off the hair drier and leads Mama to sit down at her station.

"Yes it is, which explains why Esmeralda might be interested in getting to him before we do," Mama says as she leans back in the malleable chair and allows Netta to work her magic. "I know she's got her hands in his arrest."

"No doubt about it. And you know she's going to come running to his rescue as soon as she can, indebting him to her for life." Netta moves the hot irons through Mama's head quickly, not needing to fully straighten her already soft tresses. Mama hates it when her hair falls flat from too much heat.

"Or longer," Mama says, meeting Netta's eyes in the mirror. I'm used to the two of them talking over my head.

"How can G be in debt to Esmeralda, and why would she help him get out of jail in the first place?" I ask, not making the connection. I open my locker and begin to organize my stuff—my locker at school needs the same type of attention.

"Because, little Jayd," Netta begins. "Esmeralda's gathering an entire army of sinister soldiers to be at her beck and call. These little fools running around her selling drugs and whatnot are her top targets."

"But Netta, why would Esmeralda need them to do her dirty work when she's got her top dog around?" I ask, now removing the boxes from the clients' shelves.

There are at least one hundred personalized boxes and they each need some serious TLC. Between my initiation, Mrs. Esop filing a law suit against me through Mama and Pam's murder we're slightly behind in our shop duties.

"Because she can, and because Rousseau needs help to do his dirty work. If you're making vampires and zombies, why not start with the natural ones we've already got in the hood?" Mama's right. She's always said black folks don't need to get caught up in the fictional vampires when we've got real ones like poverty and addiction to contend with on a daily basis.

"That reminds me," I say, easing into my dream confession. "I had a dream about Pam yesterday.

"That happens a lot when spirits are attempting to crossover," Netta says, admiring her skills as Mama primps her fresh do in the mirror.

"What was the dream about?" Mama asks.

"Well, I was here alone and Pam was in the back knocking on the screen door. Rousseau was after her and she said to give you the message that only you can help her. Oh, and her eyes were pitch black and she couldn't come inside for some reason. Too weird."

Before I can replace the first dozen boxes in one of the five floor length cabinets dedicated to the clients, Mama and Netta are right behind me.

"Why didn't you tell me about this sooner?" Mama asks, taking the boxes from my hands and setting them down on the table closest to us.

"Did you look her directly in the eye?" Netta asks, feeling my forehead with the back of her hand. What the hell?

"No, I don't think so," I say. "It was still dark outside."

They force me to take a seat at Netta's station and check me out from head to toe. I doubt I'll ever get used to this type of occasional reaction from my spiritual guardians. After several minutes of me repeating the details of the dream, Mama and Netta ease up satisfied that I'm okay for the time being.

"I'm sorry I didn't tell you about it yesterday. There was just so much going on and I figured since I didn't come back blind or anything like that it was just a dream." Usually when the dream is extremely important I get hurt in some sort of way. I've awakened with more bruises and cuts than I care to remember.

"The fact that she was pregnant in your dream disturbs me more than Esmeralda making her a spiritual zombie."

There's that word again. With Misty turning into whatever animal she's mimicking and Emilio right there with here, I'm over Esmeralda's growing supernatural circus.

Mama signals for me to rise from her seat and I obey, happy to get back to work.

"It was just a part of the dream," I explain. "To me the worst part was her dark eyes and grey skin. It was freaky." A chill comes over me at the sheer thought of the nightmare.

"Jayd, you don't have simple dreams," Mama says, her green eyes glowing. "You never know what they truly mean if you don't ask and consult the spirit book. I don't care how early or late it is, write it down in your journal immediately and do your research."

"That's what your journal's there for," Netta says, reminding me of the instructions that came with my personal spirit book when they first presented it to me. That's why I keep it in the car—my life always has some drama popping off.

"Esmeralda's waged war in the streets as well as in the spirit houses across Los Angeles County. I hear she's even called in some of the Houngans and Mambos, or head priest and priestesses, in Haiti on Rousseau's side," Netta says, matter-of-factly.

I know Mama and Netta have hit the pavement to gather all the information they can on Hector's botanica and spiritual family in Lynwood. His storefront happens to be down the street from my father's house. Maybe I'll take a trip to see him soon and do a little investigating of my own.

When Mama turned down Hector's offer to become the head of his house after his wife fell ill, he simply went next door and Esmeralda gladly accepted. Things haven't been the same since. Before Hector came along we had Esmeralda right where we wanted her: humbled. With this new surge of loyal followers, Esmeralda's growing in both strength and popularity: a bad combination.

"And it's apparent that Esmeralda's still trying to take over your dreams, Jayd," Mama says. "No matter what, don't give your mind over to fear and get your sleep. You've got to keep your mind strong and as drama-free as possible to beat that wench at her own game."

If it were that simple I would have eliminated Esmeralda and all other forms of drama from my life a long time ago.

"I would love to get more sleep," I say, returning the last row of boxes to their respective shelves. I'll get started on the laundry next. Hopefully after I finish washing I can get back to my mom's apartment and braid at least one head. I saw a couple of styles in my magazine that I want to try on Shawntrese.

"You've got to find a way to get it in," Netta says, running her fingers through Mama's hair, pleased with her work as always. "The wrong thoughts can be toxic to your health. If you keep your dreams to yourself it's tantamount to poisoning your mind."

"Yeah, but my reality can also keep me from sleeping at night. Besides, there are times I'd rather not dream, if you know what I mean."

Netta and Mama both look at me and sigh. I know my elders feel me, but they have little sympathy for my sometimes-impatient attitude toward my gift of sight.

"Jayd, don't think of your dreams as simply visions and premonitions, which they also are, of course. They're interactions with your subconscious mind; a type of communion with the alternate reality, if you will."

Netta spins Mama's chair around to face the mirror. Mama eyes her beautiful reflection. I catch her green glow in the mirror as she locks onto my eyes and communicates with me like only she can.

"Oh Jayd, there's so much more to reality than what you see when you're supposedly awake," Mama says, easing the tension in my mind. "Lucky for us our ancestors are the only mastermind team we need."

"Mastermind team?" I ask, unable to fold the towel in my hands as Mama continues her mental prodding.

Netta rolls her eyes at my naïveté and continues to primp Mama's hair.

"Yes, child. Your mastermind is a group of wise spirits whom you can call on when you need help, improvement, or just plain old support," my grandmother says, easing her way out of my mind. "You can interact with them however you wish. They are, after all, present only in your mind and will help you in any way you ask."

It sounds more like imaginary friends than a wise team to me, but I wouldn't dare say that out loud.

"That Napoleon Hill was an interesting white man, yes he was," Netta says, clamping Mama's hair between the iron curlers before repeating the same motion, but this time curling the ends of her hair in the hot tool before moving on to the next section. "That book he wrote back in the thirties, *Think and Grow Rich* was the truth, you hear me? Girl, it was the truth!"

Mama pulls her head away from her best friend and glares at her in shear annoyance. Mama doesn't like it when Netta—her sole hairdresser—gets too excited while doing her hair and I don't blame her. Even the most skilled stylist can slip up. If you ask me, Netta's enthusiasm is one of her most endearing qualities. Her spunky attitude and love of life is what makes her so loveable.

"Netta, black people knew the power of thinking our way out of situations way before he wrote it down," Mama says, relaxing back into her chair as Netta reclaims Mama's soft tresses. "We've always called on our ancestors for help, and they've always answered."

"Yes, but Lynn Mae you must admit that Hill wrote it all down in such a palatable way. Even people who aren't looking for the information will read it in his books and get it. I love it!"

"I don't have to admit a damned thing, Netta," Mama says, tilting her head to the right so Netta can work on the other side.

Netta sucks her teeth at her best friend's comment. They go back and forth like this all of the time. Their type of sisterhood is what I wish I could have with my girls, but it seems like the bond might skip my generation. My mom and her best friends—who I call my aunties—have been tight since diapers, as they like to say. I wish I had one friend I knew happily for that long.

"So you mean to tell me that if I call on Josephine Baker she'll come to me in my dreams and chat?" I've always wanted to ask the infamous black performer how she danced around topless in a banana skirt for white men and women to gawk at with a smile on her face. After I learned about her in drama class last year I found a photo of her and placed it on my shrine. If there was ever an Oshune woman, she's it.

"Yes, but even more than that," Mama says. "You can summon her ashe and her advice."

"Seriously," Netta agrees. "And the person doesn't have to be an ancestor. It can be anyone."

Mama nods in agreement, almost as hyped about the topic as Netta is.

"The benefit of having the gift of sight like we do is that if they're also blessed with certain talents we can borrow those talents, too," Mama says.

If they're right about this—and I don't doubt that they are—I've been sleeping on this tool, and so have a lot of people I know. It's one thing to have the power of sight like we Williams' women do, but if anyone can summon a mastermind crew, why don't they?

"Powerful. Simply magnificent," Netta says, this time in a quiet yet equally hyped tone. "I've always envied Madame C.J. Walker's ability to turn pressing hair into a million dollar business when many black people were still enslaved. That woman is on my mastermind list all day, every day."

That explains how Netta's Never Nappy Beauty Shop is still thriving in the middle of Compton, California where shops like CoCo's have taken over. Netta and Mama only deal with natural products and nothing synthetic—no weaves, extensions or anything else they deem as toxic. We make all of our own products, choose our clientele carefully and rarely accept new clients. They've been here for over thirty years and aren't going anywhere anytime soon.

"Our great, great ancestor Califia is one of my most formidable mastermind participants," Mama says, checking Netta's progress in the mirror. "She taught me how to see people's thoughts like a projector image. She can mimic any action in front of her; see the next three steps ahead. I hate playing her in chess during our mental meetings. If she sees any move in your thoughts she'll block it, throwing you completely off in the process. Her gift is one of my favorites to borrow."

Damn, I wish I had that skill. I need to see about summoning Califia through my dreams like I do Maman's and my mom's powers. Lord knows I could use some help seeing my way through this mess with Jeremy as well as in beating Esmeralda at her own game. I guess I better get to work on putting together a mastermind team of my own. And, while I'm at it I need to keep better records of my dreams. It's something about putting things down on paper that makes them seem more powerful, and I'm gong to need all the power I can get.

"Just read the damn letter, Jayd."
-Nellie
Drama High, volume 1: The Fight

Chapter 4
PAPER

It feels nice walking up the block this time of evening. It's mid October and the air is a bit chillier than it was last month, but I can still get away with wearing a pair of shorts and a hoody. If I were in the South Bay I'd be freezing my legs off by now. I was glad to leave Drama High behind when I left campus a few hours ago. Avoiding Jeremy all week was the hardest thing I've ever done. I still have very real feelings for him, but we're just not seeing eye-to-eye on his love of all things illegal. Eventually we'll have to talk about what we want to do, but right now I can't deal with any more heat.

After dealing with G's arraignment on Monday and being Nellie's chauffeur on Tuesday, I spent the rest of the week catching up on schoolwork and my clients' heads. I'm glad Mama and Netta gave me the afternoon off to get myself situated. Besides, they've been at the church almost every evening to meet with other concerned members of the neighborhood. I could've stayed and caught up on the cleaning duties but I don't want to be at the shop alone, especially not after my dream with Pam and her black eyes.

Mrs. Nguyen and her husband have been running The Right Stop liquor store for as long as my mom's lived in Inglewood. It's more than a convenience spot; it's the neighborhood everything market. From rolling papers to milk to hair beads, Mrs. Nguyen's got everything we could want within walking distance under one roof.

"Jayd, how are you?" Mrs. Nguyen asks from behind the bulletproof glass counter. After the last shooting I witnessed on Labor Day last year, they improved their security system, complete with a rent-a-cop outside of the front door and a pit bull on the back porch.

"I'm good. Just need some hair supplies and chips to hold me over until dinner." There's always a need for *Lays* in our apartment.

Shawntrese and her boyfriend have become my best clients in this area. They've been responsible for the majority of my referrals, too. One of which is his daughter, Chrystal, whose hair I'm braiding in twenty minutes. If her crown is anything like her daddy's, it'll be the last thing that I do tonight. Thankfully my Saturday schedule's already packed insuring a nice weekend profit.

I walk through the narrow aisles to the back wall where all of the hair products are lined up. I don't normally braid little girls' hair and need to stock up on pretty beads and whatnot if I'm going to make this a regular part of my hustle. The door buzzer rings indicating another patron has entered the premises, and she's a hot mess. I recognize her from around the block.

I make eye contact with her and keep it moving. The last thing I need is some drama with a female in my mom's neighborhood. It's one thing to bother me at school, but I have too many clients around here and can't afford for hating chicks to mess with my paper.

"Hey, ain't you that chick who be doing hair?" she asks.

"Yeah. Jayd," I say, picking out five large packs of multi-colored beads and a few bags of rubber bands. I hope Shawntrese knows she's going to be helping put these things in Chrystal's hair.

"Can you do my son's braids?" she asks, referring to the little boy standing behind her. "He's looking raggedy as shit and I ain't got time to hook it up."

She's about to bust soon with his little brother or sister. I guess she didn't want to be bothered with maternity clothes. Her sweats are rolled under her exposed belly and her t-shirt barely covers her large navel. Mickey wasn't quite this cavalier when she was pregnant but close enough.

"Yeah, I can try and fit you it in tomorrow afternoon." I don't know how but I should be able to squeeze a few braids in his head in between clients if all rolls smoothly. When one person is late my whole day is thrown off. "Here's my number." I take one of my business cards out and pass it to her. I need to have some more made but have to stack up my cheddar first. New clients are just the way to get that done.

"Aight, bet. My name's Channel. Say hi to Jayd, Jason."

Jason looks at me hard like if I take one step toward him he's going to kick me in the shins. I hope he melts a little once I get my hands in his hair. Maybe I'll ask Mama for a recipe to cool a child's head when in my chair. I don't want to have to wrestle a five year old to the ground to do his hair.

"It's nice to meet you," I say. "See y'all tomorrow."

After paying for my items I leave the store ready to get my Friday night started. Hopefully I'll sleep better than I have all week. Pam came to me again in my dreams repeating the same mantra from three days ago. I told Mama and Netta at the shop yesterday and they just told me to write it down, as usual. I've done more writing in my spirit journal than I did when I was first initiated over the summer. If I keep it up I can have a book of my own by the time I graduate from high school in June.

"I think that's the point," my mom says as I walk through the front door. She's wearing her *Gazelle* shades while checking the mail. I'm sure her fiancé, Karl's got something lovely planned for the weekend.

"Mom, we're going to have to talk about the misuse of your gift of sight." I shut the door closed and give her a hug.

"It's nice to see you, too, little girl. Did you bring me something back?"

"I didn't know you were going to be here," I say, setting the black plastic bag down on the dining room table.

On cue, Shawntrese opens her door across the hall and taps on ours. It's nearly impossible to sneak in this building.

"Hey, girl," I say, letting Shawntrese and my new client inside.

"And who's this cutie," my mom says aloud, but in my head I can feel she's not too pleased with a child in her peaceful abode.

"This is Chrystal, Leroy's baby girl," Shawntrese says prompting the shy child to greet us. I'll take a quiet kid over an ornery one like Jason any day.

My mom shakes her hand and smiles. "How old are you, baby?"

"I'm six," Chrystal says, holding up five fingers. My mom and I exchange a knowing look: most of the kids around here are behind academically.

"She just had a birthday." Shawntrese takes Chrystal by the hand and leads her toward the dining room.

"Shawntrese, can you grab a couple of those telephone books and put them in the chair for her?" I ask, pointing to the large books under the dining room table. At Netta's shop we have several sets bound with duct tape for occasional use. If I'm going to have small clients I guess I'll have to do the same thing.

"Well, I've got to hit the road. Karl's meeting me in Beverly Hills for our dance lessons." They've been taking various dance classes in preparation for their wedding in a few months. I think my mom's leaning toward salsa.

"Jayd, do I have to remind you that this isn't a full-service hair salon?" my mom yells into my mind. *"If you're going*

to be doing kids' hair you'll have to start going to your clients' houses, girl. I'm not having a bunch of bay-bays running all up in my space."

"*I know, mom. I'll figure it out,*" I say, attempting to focus on the child's head in front of me. Just like her daddy, she's got a head full to manage.

"*Okay, Jayd. Remember, if that little crumb snatcher breaks a damned thing in my house it's coming out of your pay,*" my mom says, walking down the stairs.

"*I love you, too.*" I wish I had an off button for my mom's mental intrusions. I know she means well most of the time, but damn. Can a sistah catch a break?

"Come on, Chrystal. Let's get your hair washed," I say, moving the chair and the little girl to the kitchen sink.

"Jayd, your phone's vibrating." Shawntrese props the phone in between my right ear and shoulder. It's Mickey. I hope she knows I'm not going anywhere tonight.

"What up, sun?" I ask, running the hot water into an old pot to pour over this child's hair.

"Not much," Mickey says. "What are you doing?"

"Braiding. You?"

"I'm watching *Kendra,*" Mickey says, popping her gum. She's found a new role model in the reality TV mom. "And then *Ice Loves Coco* is coming on."

"Mickey, I have to go," I say, securing the white towel around Chrystal's neck before I rinse her hair. "I just started a new head."

"Okay. Call me when you're done. Nellie wants to go to some party in Redondo Beach and my mom said she'll watch the baby." I think my girl is bored and I know Rah's just about lost his patience with his latest houseguest.

"Mickey, have you talked to Nigel?" I ask, knowing he's not in the mood to chat with Mickey.

I hope she admits her wrongdoings and fixes this shit before it gets completely out of hand. I already turned back the hands of time when her ex-man shot Nigel, but I can't do the same thing again—or at least I don't think I can nor would I want to. That was a specific circumstance to get Nickey here safely. This new drama is on some other shit that I want no part of.

"Nah, I ain't talked to that fool," Mickey says, disappointed. "He's still tripping and I could really care less at this point."

Who can blame Nigel for tripping hard? He sacrificed everything for our girl and her daughter. She's completely in the wrong for this shit right here, but Nigel does love her and I'd hate to see them call it quits when they have so much responsibility to each other and the baby. Granted, Nickey Shantae is not Nigel's daughter—technically—but he did sign the birth certificate and gave her his last name, officially making him the daddy in the court's eyes.

"Well, I'm going over Chase's house tomorrow if you want to come," I say, rinsing out the mango shampoo ready to put the coconut conditioner on Chrystal's hair. The child's almost asleep she's so relaxed. "I'm sure he wants to see the baby."

"What about me? He needs to bring his ass over here and check for his girl before it's too late. This shit is all wrong if you ask me."

Is Mickey serious? She's the one who committed the major violation, not Nigel and she's still acting like the Queen Bee. My God, this girl is a trip and then some.

"Jayd," Nellie says, taking over the call. "Can you come out tonight, please? ASB is having their first party of the year at *The Cheesecake Factory*. You know it's going to be fierce. Did I mention they're considering me for the cheer squad?"

"Nellie, if you recall the reason there's a spot available on the damned squad is because they kicked me off," I say, reminding my girl of the truth as it is, not how she wants to see it.

"Jayd, that's all water under the bridge now," Nellie says, overly excited about being back in the good graces of the crew she so desperately wants to be a part of. "And besides, it's free food. Come on, girl. I know it's your favorite restaurant.

She's right about that but duty calls. Chrystal's hair is going to take me all night. "Maybe next time, Nellie. I've got my hands full over here."

"Whatever, Jayd." Nellie passes the cell back to Mickey who sounds equally exasperated.

"Jayd, you need to have a little fun. All you do is work and study. It's our senior year and your missing it."

Mickey does have a point. I'm going to graduate in less than eight months and I have yet to have a wild high school experience. Not that a free dinner qualifies as wild, but I do need to have a little more fun. Too bad I can't start this evening.

"I'll get on that as soon as I make this money," I say, running the hot water for Chrystal's final rinse. If I'm lucky she'll sleep through the entire braiding process. "Holla."

I hang up my phone and place it on the kitchen counter. My girls are right: I need to enjoy my senior year of high school before it's all said and done. And in order to do that, I've got to get my money right. Besides, I'm still dealing with Nigel's mom suing me, and Esmeralda's constant bull. I wish I could sit around and watch mindless television like my friends, but shit is real around here.

It's been a busy Saturday and I'm glad for it. I managed to get through six heads before the day was done and still get to the shop to help out Netta and Mama. It's evening time and I'm ready to chillax with my crew even if my girls will be missing. They opted to go to yet another ASB party instead of hang out at Chase's house with me. I hope this isn't the beginning of the end of our crew as we know it. If it is, who gets custody of me? If I'm forced to choose between Mickey and Nigel—or Chase and Nellie—I don't know what I'll do.

Mama and Netta have been busy preparing for the big neighborhood meeting at church tomorrow after Daddy's sermon. They've visited G every day this week who's completely resistant to any outside assistance. I haven't had a chance to talk to Mickey in depth about her reentering a relationship with G, but I will as soon as I can. She's lost her mind if she thinks dude can just forgive her for leaving him for Nigel.

I also need to speak with Nigel about his Mama's latest stunt. I know Mama's distracted with Pam's murder, but as soon as she's back on it, Mrs. Esop's going to be in for it and I don't want to see her get hurt. Maybe if Nigel takes his stubborn ass home his mom will back off.

"There's my girl," Nigel says, looking like a porcupine exploded on top of his head. "I'm ready for you, baby." Nigel points to his wild hair and I can't help but laugh at my boy.

"Yeah you are," I say, placing my hair bag down on Chase's bedroom floor ready to work.

Nigel's made himself right at home with his shit everywhere. The house has five more empty bedrooms but he seems to be bunking right here on the couch.

"I got next," Chase says without taking his eyes away from his *PS2* for a moment. I can tell they've been playing this war game all day long by the glazed look in both of their eyes.

Nigel has football practice every day after school except on Fridays, which are game nights. The team also has meetings on Saturday mornings and Nigel spends the rest of the weekend chilling to make up for his dedication. Homecoming's in a couple of weeks and I know recruiters will be out in full-effect in an attempt to woo Nigel away from UCLA, but we all know he's made his decision. Hell, with P. Diddy's son as one of his teammates next year I wouldn't budge, either.

"What's new, girl?" Nigel says, making himself comfortable on the floor in front of me. Before I get into a comfortable braid position I need to let him in on our legal drama.

"Your mama is suing my Mama; that's what," I say, tossing the legal papers into Nigel's lap.

"Say what?" Chase says, looking away from the screen as stunned as I was when Mrs. Esop served us at Netta's shop a couple of weeks ago.

"What are you talking about?" Nigel asks. He unfolds the long papers and glances at the words in bold print. "Plaintiff. Defendant. Are you serious?"

"Hell yeah I'm serious," I say, parting his hair with my fingers. I've got my work cut out for me this evening, but it's cool. Nigel always pays and tips me well above average. "Does it look like she's joking?"

"Damn, that's some cold shit right there, no doubt." Chase glances over Nigel's shoulder, reading the document word for word.

I still can't believe Nigel moved out of Rah's house and opted to stay all the way in Palos Verdes. I know my boys are cool, but I'd never thought I'd see the day that Nigel would up and leave his hood to move to the "Beverly Hills by the beach", as the members of this elite community call it.

"Jayd, I don't know what to say. I knew she was pissed about the ball and the dress and all that, but not this angry." Nigel refolds the papers and regretfully passes them back to me. "It's not like she can't afford the loss."

"Exactly. But suing my grandmother over a gown is beyond frivolous, and we can't afford it." I don't want to remind Nigel that Mama has a way of fixing things beyond the law's reach, but that's exactly where this situation's headed if Mrs. Esop doesn't back down.

"You know, you should talk to my mom about this," Chase says, returning to his game. "It's right up her alley." Chase is back to calling his mother mom and it sounds good. At least my spiritual work for he and his family wasn't in vain.

"What do you mean?" I ask, glancing at the court documents. I still can't believe this shit.

"You know my mom helped David start his practice," Chase says, referring to his estranged father. "In all reality, it's their practice. Dude just likes to act like everything's his, but without my mom's contacts and savvy he wouldn't be anywhere. That's why I hope she takes David for everything he's worth and more."

Damn, Mrs. Carmichael's running it like that? I had no idea.

"I can't ask her to help me with all she's dealing with," I say, returning the documents to my bag.

"Jayd, I don't know everything that's been going on between you and my mom but I'm sure she'd be more than happy to return the favor," Chase says, smiling in between video game fatalities.

"Chase is right," Nigel says, wincing as I comb his hair out. "Knowing my mom, you're going to need your own attorney and a good one. She loves drama and more than that, she loves to win."

I know Nigel's right. I need an attorney who can fight like his mom's team, not Daddy's lawyer friends who deal with mostly criminal trials.

"I'll think about it," I say, attempting to check my emotions and focus on the task at-hand. Between Esmeralda and Mrs. Esop, my mind's too crowded with bull.

"You have to learn to ask for help when you need it. The people who love you would be more than happy to help a sistah out when in need, ya feel me?" Nigel says, bending his head back with a huge smile across his face displaying his perfectly straight teeth.

"For real, shawdy," Chase says, in his best southern accent. "Let's holla at mom's and see what she has to say about the whole thing. She's really been on her A game since she filed for divorce, reading legal journals and studying and shit. I'm proud of her," Chase says, overly excited about his mother's healing. He pauses the game and stands up, towering over my five-foot frame. "I'm sure she'd love to take your case on just for the hell of it. David will have to find another job after my mom's done with his ass."

"If you insist," I say, reclaiming the papers and following my boys out of the room.

We head downstairs where Mrs. Carmichael's on the computer with piles of paper around her. It's a welcome change from her usual stance by the bar with a glass of liquor in one hand and a cigarette in the other. There's nothing like a cheating husband with a pregnant mistress to sober a chick up real quick. I'm glad she's back on her grind. We need more sharp women attorneys in the world.

"Hey, sweetie. Hungry?" Mrs. Carmichael asks her son without looking up. Her red hair's pulled back in a ponytail and she has on glasses—a look I've never seen on her before and it suits her well.

"Always," Chase says, rubbing his flat stomach. "But before we eat Jayd wants to run something by you if you don't mind," Chase says, kissing his mom on the cheek. I guess he finally realizes that she has his back like no one else in the world ever will, blood or not.

"Oh dear, I didn't even notice you were here," Mrs. Carmichael says, winking at me. "Please help yourselves to dinner. I had it catered from *Boston's Market* so there's plenty to go around. And Nigel, don't be shy. Our house is your home now, too."

Wow, she's in a damn good mood. I'll have to let Mama know that the Loving Home tincture is where it's at.

"Thanks, Mrs. C," Nigel says, rubbing his hands together, ready to throw down. Nigel heads toward the kitchen with Chase right behind him.

"So, what's up Miss Jackson?" Mrs. Carmichael asks, giving me her undivided attention.

"Well, the short and sweet of it is that Nigel's mom is suing me for reimbursement of my couture gown she had custom designed for the debutante ball."

"This is the same ball you did not want to attend, correct?" Mrs. Carmichael asks, flipping a page in her yellow legal pad over to a clean sheet.

"Yes, ma'am."

Mrs. Carmichael points to an empty seat across from hers where I sit as directed.

She's taking this lawyer thing seriously. Something tells me I'm in good hands with her. Mama never talked about her full association with Mrs. Carmichael outside of her trying to help her have a baby back in the day, but I bet there's more to the story now that I know her true profession outside of being a rich housewife in PV.

"Did you at anytime request a designer gown for said event?"

"No, ma'am. I didn't even want to participate, but she made me in exchange for her appearing at Nigel and Mickey's baby shower," I say, recalling the twisted agreement on behalf of Mickey.

"So, basically you entered into a verbal agreement with Teresa Esop which she initiated to benefit a third party," Mrs. Carmichael says. "Did you fulfill your end of the bargain?"

"Yes, I did to the best of my abilities," I say, recalling my unexpected meltdown. "I fell ill the night of the ball. The gown was ruined as a result, but I showed up."

Mrs. Carmichael looks into my eyes and knows there's more to the story. I can't divulge all of the mystical events of that night; that I was taken over by my great-grandmother's spirit, pulled into the ocean's current and reborn as an initiate to Oshune. No, the personal details of the night in question aren't necessary but I'm sure she catches my drift.

"Jayd, please tell Lynn Mae that I'm on the case. Don't worry your pretty little head about Teresa Esop. I'll get started on drafting a letter of rebuttal countersuing her for harassment and breach of contract," Mrs. Carmichael says, flipping her *MacBook Pro* open. I wish I could afford my own computer. "Do you have the initial summons?"

"Here it is," I say, handing Mrs. Carmichael the legal documents. She looks all too eager to help a sistah out and I'm grateful for her sassy spunk.

"Excellent. I'll make a copy of these and of the letter once I'm done. Don't lose any sleep over this, my dear." Mrs. Carmichael pats my hand and smiles, reassuring me that it's all going to be okay.

"I know you have a lot on your plate," I say, unaccustomed to being the one in need of counseling. "I appreciate you taking the time to hear me out." I rise from my seat ready to get back to work.

Alia should be on her way over to watch a movie. I wish I could stay and chill for the rest of the night but Mama's requested that I spend the night at her house. We have to be up early in the morning to attend church with Daddy. She knows I'll be late if left to my own vices. Mama has a full day of activities outlined for us tomorrow and it starts with sunrise service.

"Jayd, you've helped me so much. I'm going to do everything I can to help you out with your situation."

"Mrs. Carmichael, thank you eventhough I know this has nothing to do with you."

"Oh, but it does, my dear. I know how sorority women work, especially when they feel betrayed. Trust me, I'll handle this. I know I may seem like a simple housewife now, but I did attend law school and still know a thing or two."

Mrs. Carmichael rises from her seat and hugs me tight.

"Thank you," I say, shocked at what a sober Mrs. Carmichael can do.

"You are most welcome, Miss Jackson. Now, go eat something and let me get back to work."

Mrs. Carmichael's husband's really in for it. Like the saying goes, if you lay down with dogs you'll wake up with fleas. By now Mr. Carmichael must be itching like the little bitch that he is. By the time she's done, Mr. Carmichael probably won't have a pot to piss in, and that's more than what he deserves.

"In this life, all roads are valid."
-Mama
Drama High, volume 10: Culture Clash

Chapter 5
THE WALKING DEAD

I arrive in Compton just before ten and the block is alive with folks hanging out. It stays relatively warm throughout the year in California but it does get chilly once the sun goes down. I glance across the back gate and notice it's busy at Esmeralda's house. The singing is loud and the drums even louder. I swear I can hear animals in the chorus but maybe that's just the lack of talent in the room. From what I saw the last time they had a bembe, there's not much freethinking in Esmeralda's house, thus the uniform hum barely audible over the pulsating percussions.

Keenan texted me four times today, each time asking when he's going to see me again. After avoiding him all week I spoke to him briefly last night. I tried to fit him into my schedule and make up for not twisting his hair, but it took all night to finish Chrystal's braids on Friday and today was equally packed. After finishing Nigel's hair a little while ago, I'm no good to anyone. I had to make some hot chocolate with cayenne pepper sprinkled on top to give me the jolt I needed to make it through the day. Forget energy drinks or espresso: Netta's Cayenne Coco is a miracle in a mug.

Speaking in miracles, I'm amazed by Mrs. Carmichael's complete makeover without the help of a television show. I've known Chase for three years and his mom's always been an alcoholic, zombie-like housewife—not the lively, smart attorney I met with this afternoon. I can't wait to tell Mama all about the new development. I also need her advice on Mickey being back with G and how to deal with the shit before it hits the fan. I'll open with the good news first because we could all use some, especially Mama.

When I open the door to the spirit room Lexi's asleep in her customary spot at the threshold while Mama's at her best in the small kitchen.

"Alaafia, Iyawo," Mama says, greeting me in traditional Yoruba language.

"Alaafia, Iyalosha." I kiss my grandmother on the cheek and walk over to the main room to change into my white clothes. I was hoping to go straight to bed after my long workday but not tonight. I've been behind on my spirit work and apparently we're taking the chance to catch me up on that and more.

"Mrs. Carmichael said to tell you that she's on the case," I say, setting my purse on one of several bookshelves lining the walls of the quaint house. My clothes are draped over the Japanese room dividers used to give some privacy in the open space.

"Excellent," Mama says. "I'm glad Lindsay's back to life. That man had her nose closed for twenty years. It's about time she got back to using the gifts God gave her before she married that jackass."

"Was she a good attorney back in the day?" I ask, stepping back into the kitchen area anxious to learn more about Chase's mom. I was very impressed with what I saw and can only imagine how she really rolls.

"Was she ever?" Mama sifts the flour and other dry ingredients in a large mixing bowl. She then directs me with her eyes to claim the wet ingredients for the batter. "Lindsay was the baddest attorney in New Orleans before David came along with his New York ass. They met during a court case so unprecedented that it made the newspapers," Mama says, her green eyes excited as she relives the memory. "When she kicked his ass up and down Canal Street David made it his mission to have Lindsay. To men like him women are to be conquered not loved, which is exactly what he did with her."

"I never even knew she was a brilliant attorney," I say, cracking the first of three eggs in a small mixing bowl. I'll add the vanilla and lemon extracts next. Mama hasn't made pound cake in a month of Sundays, as Netta would say. I hope it's for us and not a client. We all need something sweet to even out the bitter ever-present in life.

"That's because Lindsay was raised to be a good, Southern girl. Her family believed women had to give up their identities once they became wives and she was no different, even if she was the sharpest lawyer I'd ever met." Mama takes the wooden spoon off of the kitchen table and taps my bowl ready to blend the ingredients. "Thank God she's out of that coma she's been living in for the past two decades. Now the healing process can finally begin."

"She was more than happy to take on the case for us, for free at that," I say, watching Mama blend the yellow batter to perfection. I can't wait to lick the spoon—being the taste tester is the best part about helping out in the kitchen. That's why my cousin, Jay and me have been Mama's helpers since childhood. I miss him now that he's a working adult. He opted out of college and decided to get two full-time jobs instead. All Jay wants to do is sleep and eat when he is home.

"Of course she was, dear," Mama says, pointing at the melted butter and cake pan for me to grease. "That's what loyal clients do. It's a two-way street as all reciprocal relationships should be."

"It's a shame it had to come down to this." I reach across the table and get to work.

"Yes, it is. But if I know one thing about women like Teresa it's that she's been planning this set up for a long time."

Sounds a lot like a few chicks I know, mainly Misty. She's always got more than one trick up her sleeve.

"Mama, why do some females make it so difficult to be friends?"

Mama turns off the mixer and looks up at me like I'm a complete stranger. I know she went through the same thing with Mrs. Esop and her sorority clique when she was in college, which is why Mama has been rogue ever since. With the exception of Netta, Mama has no friends. Associates, but not friends.

"Jayd, have you listened to a word I've said for the past seventeen years of your life?" Mama asks, pouring the mix into the coated pan. I can't wait until she's finished.

"Yes, ma'am," I say, taking a towel from the kitchen drawer and drying the clean dishes in the strainer.

"I know, baby. It's difficult to understand why people would spend their energy plotting and scheming when they could just as easily act in kindness, but most people would rather see you cry than smile. It's not your issue. All you need to do is cover your heart like the good book says instead of wearing it on your sleeve and you'll be all right." Mama and I both look at the large spirit book on the kitchen counter and smile.

"But why pretend?" I ask, tired of the games chicks play. Mrs. Esop's so out of my league that I can't even comprehend how to deal with her petty ass. "I have no time for fronting."

Mama looks at me and rolls her eyes at my street vernacular. Satisfied with her creation, Mama opens the oven, places the cake inside and promptly sets the timer.

"Because that's the nature of the beast, Jayd. And the beast is real." Mama closes the oven and breathes a sigh of relief, tired from the long week. "The sooner you woman up and recognize that good intentions pave the road to hell, the sooner you can turn around and head in the other direction."

"Mama, how am I supposed to know who to help and who to leave alone?" After placing the last dish in the strainer I take a seat across from Mama.

She takes my hands palms up in hers and reads the tiny lines. Her honey brown skin's flawless unlike a lot of people her age. "Unfortunately baby, most people don't mean you well. The problem with y'all young folks is that you want to be everyone's friend instead of realizing that friendship is priceless and not to be given away so easily. Love the people who love you and avoid the rest like the bad seeds that they are."

The drumbeats from next door grow more intense and cause Lexi to growl from her perch outside the door.

"What's going on over there?" I ask, interrupting our psychic session.

Mama's eyes begin to shine as she focuses on the house next door. We can't see everything from the window nor do we need to. Anyone with a soul can feel the evil going on.

"Let's go inside, Jayd," Mama says, calming her green glow. "I'll send Jay back out here when the cake's done."

"Okay." I claim my things from the main room ready to lay down myself.

"Grab the spirit book, sweetie," Mama says, turning off the lights.

I do as I'm told and follow Mama through the back yard lit only by the full moon. Daddy was supposed to replace the porch light outside the spirit room weeks ago but hasn't even purchased the bulbs yet.

"To answer your question," Mama whispers. "Esmeralda's creating an army of blind allegiance to her and only her through the Orisha community. She wants to run all of the spirit houses on the west side, but I have a feeling it's more than that."

"Wow," I say, unable to take it all in.

"When Esmeralda married Hector's ile she also married the spirits of Rousseau's animals with the spirits of her followers making a living voodoo doll, if you will."

"Mama, how do you know all of this?" I ask, shocked at how calm Mama's being.

"With the exception of working at the shop, Netta and I have been in the spirit room since yesterday working on finding out Esmeralda's plan." We step quietly through the grass with Lexi leading the way. "All we know is that she's used Rousseau to summon my father's spirit and help create the zombies and shape shifters. I have to find a way to stop her before it's too late."

"Can't we just make a potion to stop them?" I ask, keeping my eyes and ears open. You never know who or what's waiting in the dark.

I can't believe Esmeralda's game is this tight. Just a couple of months ago I was crushing her with my newfound power of sight. The tables sure have turned quickly. I'm still stuck on the fact that zombies are real. I don't want to deal with any of them even if they're not like the ones on television. My run-in with Pam's vacant eyes—now permanently etched into my memory—was more than enough contact with the walking dead for me.

"It doesn't work like that," Mama says, lifting her long skirt and stepping over the exposed tree roots. "They were initiated by Esmeralda and she's the keeper of their soperas. Without them I can't influence their heads."

Mama reminds me that I haven't cleaned my vessels this week. They each hold the ashe of the orishas and also the ashe of their owners' heads. Mine are at my mom's house on the small shrine I placed in the living room corner. I took better care of my shrines when they were here.

"Misty and Emilio were initiated like I was, right?" I ask, eager to help. If that means crippling my enemies in the process, so be it. "Maybe I can find a way to get into their heads without using their vessels."

"No, Jayd. Don't mess with them," Mama says, stopping in her tracks before reaching the back door. She turns around and faces me. "They were not properly married to their spiritual heads but instead to Esmeralda's will. She can manipulate them to do whatever she needs them to do and be whoever she wants them to be. And with Rousseau summoning his godfather—my father—on her behalf, who knows what kind of demented thoughts they've already managed to put in their heads."

"Good evening, ladies," Rousseau says, appearing at the back gate adjacent to the same driveway where Pam's body was found. "Did I hear someone call my name?"

Lexi charges and stops short of the gate, growling fiercely at our unwelcomed visitor. I feel like doing the same thing.

"Returning to the scene of your latest crime, I see," I say, stepping toward the gate behind Lexi.

"Get in the house, now," Mama says, looking at me like I've lost my mind for speaking to Rousseau. Mama ignores the intrusive neighbor, ushering Lexi and me through the door. Once we're safely inside the kitchen, Mama smacks me on the back of my arm like she used to do when I was a little girl.

"Ouch!" I say, rubbing the sore spot. "What was that for?"

"That was for being a smart-ass," Mama says, slitting her eyes at me. "Whatever you do from now on, don't engage he or Esmeralda. Ever."

"I have a feeling you're not telling me something," I say, following her through the living room toward her bedroom.

I nod what's up to my cousin, Jay and my uncles. It's still early for them to go out. Bryan's the only one missing because he's at his weekend night gig deejaying for the local independent radio station. Bryan doesn't get paid for his show, Night Science, which is dedicated to conscious music across various genres. Bryan loves that job almost as much as he loves his girlfriend.

"There's a lot you don't know, which is exactly why you need to watch your step." Mama removes her sandals and sits down on the corner of her bed. I follow suit and sit down on mine ready to listen. "When Esmeralda lost her spiritual house in New Orleans she also lost her powers to influence animals the same way she used to when we were younger. It's a divine gift, indeed. I know what Lexi's saying because we communicate in various ways, but to talk to her like we're talking now is beyond my scope of understanding."

"I feel you," I say, touching the spirit book on my bed. "I can't imagine what it would be like to constantly hear animals' voices in my head. The sample I got when I saw as she does a while back was a complete trip." No wonder Esmeralda's one step away from the insane asylum.

"When it was just Esmeralda over there I could handle it. But now that she's got her partner in both crime and in life back from the undead, it's going to take a lot more to tame her wild ass," Mama says, staring at Lexi making herself comfortable in the hallway separating Mama's room, Daddy's room and the bathroom.

"Mama, why don't we just fight fire with fire," I say, recalling one of my visions where Maman's dress caught on fire when her husband walked into the room. My great-grandfather's head belongs to Shango, just like G's. Everything he does is hot.

"Never that, Jayd. We are sweet water children, daughters of Oshune. We don't need fire or their type of evil to win this battle."

"Then what do we need?" I ask, settling into my pillow.

Mama looks at the shrine next to her bed before claiming the mail from the nightstand in between our beds. She doesn't have to voice her frustration; her eyebrows always crinkle at the sight of bills.

"What I've learned from the ancestors is that through it all you keep going. No matter what you never loose faith—period. And that's what we have to do."

"But Mama, that's not an answer."

"We have to trust in the process, Jayd," Mama says, visibly exhausted. "How many times have I told you that? The answer will come as long as we do the work."

"Yes, ma'am," I say, ready to drift off.

I promised Rah I'd hook he and Rahima's hair up tomorrow after church. His younger brother, Kamal should be home for the weekend. He started middle school this year and rarely comes back to Los Angeles to hang with his brother and baby mama drama. Who can blame him? There's peace at their grandparent's house on the other side of Compton. Maybe Rah should consider moving back there for a while to get away from Sandy's crazy ass. It could also help with the financial pinch he's been feeling since his mom stopped paying her half of the bills and rent.

The alarm from the oven in the backhouse sounds loudly and the neighborhood dogs respond. We can smell the pound cake through the bedroom window. I hope Mama lets me taste it in the morning.

"Jay, go and get the cake out of the oven and turn it off, please," Mama says out of the opened bedroom door.

Jay's the only man Mama allows in the spirit room alone. Bryan can go sometimes but has a habit of borrowing incense and candles from the supply cabinet, which works Mama's nerves.

Mama replaces the mortgage payment in the neatly opened envelope and puts it on the edge of her dresser before climbing into bed. Daddy will pick it up when he comes home. This is my grandparent's system: It allows them to communicate once a day without being too intimate. In their brief conversation they'll exchange important household information such as necessary groceries and other bills, chores and a brief discussion on children and neighbors in that order, every time. Daddy might ask me about my day, but usually I just sit on the corner of my bed and stare at whatever's on television. It must be uncomfortable for Daddy to stand at the threshold of what used to be his room, but that's the way it's been since I can remember.

I can't imagine Jeremy and I ever becoming that distant but it feels like that's the direction we're headed. Hell, I never thought I'd date a white boy in the first place but I did, and I fell in love with him—hard. Lord knows I want to help Jeremy in any way that I can but it's his family's disease that's got him thinking his way of life is okay. I hope Jeremy can find his way back to us before I completely move on.

"Speak for your ancestors and they will take care of you."
-Mama
Drama High, volume 10: Culture Clash

Chapter 6
BLOOD TIES

Sometimes I forget just how many people attempt to fit into the crammed sanctuary at First AME Church of Compton. Mama, Netta and I decided to dress in yellow and white honoring both Oshune and Pam's spirit. Had I known I was going to end up wearing everyone else's scent I wouldn't have bothered putting on my own perfume. I wish I had time to take a shower before I came to work but we all drove straight to the shop. Clients started arriving at noon and have been coming steadily for the last six hours.

Mama and Netta are wrapping up the last sister's hair now sending her home with a few samples of our latest products. All the proceeds from the Heavenly Healing line will go to Pam's funeral first, and then G's defense fund. Mama's meeting at the church was good for that and for finding a team of lawyers to volunteer in the meantime. Mama promised they would eventually get paid for their services and the church congregation backed her up.

Daddy's sermon was very inspiring, so much so that he called the entire congregation to service. He walked straight out of the church and down the street to all of the other churches of various denominations to ask them to join us for the early morning outing, and they did. We walked several blocks until our feet hurt. Bryan, who was at home with the rest of my uncles and Jay, said we looked like Jehovah's witnesses. Mama said we looked like God's soldiers, handed Jay a tambourine and made them all join us on our trek.

"Jayd, you're free to leave, honey. It's been a long day," Netta says, kissing me on the forehead.

"Yes, baby. Get some good rest," Mama says, following her best friend into the back office.

I finish sweeping the floor before preparing to head out. I'm glad tomorrow's Columbus Day, even if I could care less about the holiday. As Mama says, only in this country can you be rewarded for getting lost and enslaving every indigenous person you encountered along the way. At least we get a day off from school. I have plenty of work to catch up on and an ASU meeting to plan. Spirit week and Homecoming are both around the corner leaving our group little time to recruit new members.

"Bye. I love y'all," I say, knowing they're in the back counting money and checking the books.

"Be safe, Jayd. Mo feran o," Mama says, sending her love in Yoruba.

My phone vibrates in my jean pocket. Every time it rings I half hope it's Jeremy but it never is. Instead, it's Rah.

"Hello," I say, hanging my work apron up in my locker and retrieving my purse from the hook. I take a quick look out of the peephole and head out the front door.

"Jayd, what up?" Rah asks. "We still on for tonight?"

"Yeah, I'll be there," I say, starting the car.

My mom's clutch has been acting funny lately. Rah said if it needs replacing he could get me a good deal on the parts and do the labor for free—yet another thing I need to save my money for.

"Cool. I'm going to drop off Kamal at my grand-parent's house. I'll holla when I'm on my way back."

"I was hoping I'd get to see him," I say, pulling away from the shop. "Tell him I said what's up."

"Bet. In a minute," Rah says, ending the call. I guess I can get some studying done in the meantime.

Mama said we need to keep the faith and the answer will come. I get that, but I also want to see if our ancestors have any advice on how to stop Esmeralda's sinister plan in this moment. We've got enough going on in our hood without her twisted bull adding to the pot. I brought the spirit book with me to look up more on my great-grandmother as well. If anyone knows how to deal with Jon Paul it's his wife, Maman.

Luckily, my mom didn't find my *Lay's* stashed away in the cupboard. They were just as good today as they would've been on Friday, which is when I originally planned to eat them. I haven't had a moment to myself in this apartment since then and am enjoying the peace and quiet as well as my readings on Maman and her favorite great-ancestor, Queen Califia. She was gangster with her style and her power of sight.

Califia was able to see through anything and anyone to reveal hidden treasures and vulnerabilities. If she was looking at the earth, she could see vaults, valuable stones and other things hidden beneath the surface. If Califia was dealing with a person she could see their intentions before they manifested. No wonder Maman liked summoning her energy. Predicting one's behavior has many advantages especially when dealing with those who want to do me harm.

The spirit book also talks about the many women in our bloodline who've either had our veve tattooed or branded on their bodies, usually on the left shoulder. From the drawings Maman left behind, Califia's brand was a gorgeous brick red color against her dark brown skin.

"That looks like it hurt," I say aloud. I don't think I'm woman enough to get a brand. I know some fraternity brothas practice the outdated method of claiming ownership on slaves and cattle. I think there's a reason tattoos have become more popular than the hot iron to skin method.

Rah probably won't be back from Compton for another hour or so. The ever-present luggage under my eyes tells me that I could use a quick nap. The spirit book will be nice and cozy on the coffee table; I'll study some more when I wake up.

"Queen Califia, he's coming for you," a young girl whispers to me. We seem to be in some sort of cave with several dozen

other people of various ages. The only light comes from the fire burning in the center of the circle of chained bodies. My ankles are bound together and my right hand is bound to the girl's left.

"It'll be okay," I say, comforting the child even though I have no idea what she's talking about.

"Aren't you scared, Queen?" I look into her big, brown eyes filled with fear.

"Scared of what?" I ask, confused about the situation.

"Of Master Cortez doing what he did to them on you."

I follow her eyes to the other Africans, all shackled and freshly branded with the letter C on their left shoulders. I feel my shoulder and notice that I haven't been burned—yet.

"There's no time to be scared, Sophia," I say, quickly assessing the situation. No matter the outcome Queen Califia wouldn't go down without a fight. "We have to fight fire with fire to defeat the evil taking over our land."

I grab the eleke around my neck with our family veve in gold hanging from the center and kiss it to my forehead. "I'll be damned if he claims my body as his property, not like this."

Tired of sitting in the near dark, I stand up forcing Sophia to also stand. I glare at the wall until my eyes begin to take on a green glow similar to Maman's. At first nothing happens, but moments later I can clearly see through the wall. Cortez and his men are searching for a new tool to brand me with. He wants to make sure he makes an example out of the dethroned Queen of California.

The other captives blankly stare at me, traumatized by the day's events. One minute they were wealthy property owners and the next violently captured by Cortez and his army. Surrendering was never an option.

"Come on," I say to Sophia, gently pulling the shackles and moving toward the flames. I take my necklace off and dangle the gold charm in the fire until it's bright red. Sophia's eyes glow with tears ready to fall.

I grit my teeth and smile. "Everything will be okay because we know who owns our souls." I lay the necklace on my left shoulder; the hot metal burns my skin adding to the stench of freshly seared flesh in the air. Rather than scream from the pain, I feel Califia's sight become stronger with each passing moment.

"Are you all right, Queen?" Sophia asks, the water in her eyes suspended as she awaits my answer.

All of the captives are staring at me as if I've just sentenced us all to death. Weren't we already dead?

"If I'm going to be claimed it'll be by my own hands, not his."

Cortez enters the space and approaches me with his new tool in hand. He spits fresh tobacco juice on the ground and advances toward Sophia and me. Ignoring my young companion's terror, Cortez grabs me by the arm and stops short of throwing us to the ground.

"What is this witchcraft you've defiled your body with?" he screams, throwing me against the stone wall with all of his strength.

Blood drips from my mouth. Sophia cries out in fear as Cortez curses our gods in his native tongue. Queen Califia knows what she's doing. I smile at my abuser, ready to give him a taste of his own medicine.

"Sir, it's glowing!" one of Cortez's soldiers exclaims, pointing at my arm. "Ay dios mio! The brand's on fire!"

Cortez opens his water canteen and pours out the entire contents onto my shoulder. Instead of quenching the fire the water fuels the flames and Califia's power.

"We will all burn to the ground before you make slaves out of us!" I say, calling my relatives to arms.

At first, the other women, men and children in the space stare on in silence, but one by one they rise to their feet in solidarity. With flames dancing all around us, we are finally set free.

My cell rings loudly and scares me half to death.

"Hello," I say groggily into my cell. How long have I been out?

"Jayd, it's Rah. Did I wake you?"

"You could say that," I say, touching my right shoulder. It feels hot much like it did in my vision a moment ago. "Are you ready for me to do your hair?"

"First me and Nigel are going to get new tats real quick. Want to roll?" Rah asks like they're going to *Ralph's* for groceries. As many tattoos as they both have I guess it is a bit like shopping to them.

"What about your hair?" I ask, suddenly aware I'm losing money to Rah's impulsive buy. "I need my ends, sun."

Rah laughs at my East coast accent but I'm serious.

"We'll take care of all that."

I think it's interesting that I just had a dream about a tattoo of sorts and now my boys are talking about going to get one. I wouldn't mind getting out of the house and doing something other than working for a change.

"Okay. Give me fifteen minutes to get over there," I say, rising from the couch and wiping the drool from my chin. I was out like a baby and grateful for it. "A quick face wash and I'll be ready to go." Thank goodness it's just my boys. If it were Keenan or Jeremy I'd have to go through a whole other process before walking outside.

"Aight. We'll see you when you get here," Rah says, hanging up.

It may not be the perfect time to drill Nigel on his feelings for Mickey but there's no time like the present. I just pray Mickey's rekindled feelings for G are a form of temporary insanity at best. If Nigel finds out that they're back together there's no telling what he'll do.

When I arrived at Rah's house my boys told me all about me how Mickey disappeared with the baby last night. I haven't talked to my girl since I couldn't go to the party with she and Nellie on Friday. This is the fifth time I've called Mickey in the past hour and she refuses to pick up the phone. I know Nellie's churching it all day with her boo so I haven't even bothered trying to reach her. Mickey has truly lost her mind this time. From what I can tell Nigel doesn't know about her and G's recent family plans. I don't want him to find out the wrong way nor do I want to be the one to tell him. Hopefully I can convince Mickey to change her mind and they'll be no need for the confession.

By the time we get to Sunset Boulevard it's packed with fly-ass whips and people walking around. I didn't know they were rolling like this on a Sunday night. Maybe it's just because of the holiday tomorrow. The only homework I have due on Tuesday is our Columbus Day history report. When is Mrs. Peterson going to give up and retire? It should be illegal to have the meanest History teacher and the most evil English teacher in the same semester.

"Nigel, Rah. What's up?" the tatted brother behind the counter says. There are mirrors lining each of the four walls allowing spectators to see the process from various angles.

Three local college girls watch as he puts a butterfly on the lower back of their friend, traditionally referred to as a "tramp stamp". I think it's cute but I can see how it got that name.

"Nothing much, Julian," Rah says, stepping into the shop ahead of us.

There are pictures of tattoos lining the mirrored walls. No piercings or jewelry like in the other spots up and down the block—Julian's Ink Spot is solely about tattoos.

"This is our girl, Jayd." Julian smiles my way and I return the gesture.

Rah approaches the station to check the progress of Julian's current client. Apparently they had an appointment. Rah hates when his time is wasted.

"What are we working on today?" Julian asks, passing the girl in the chair a hand mirror. She looks at her reflection and smiles.

"The Adinkra symbol, Akoben on our forearms," Nigel says, flexing his tight arms for all to see. "It's our new business logo."

The girls perk up at Nigel's muscular display. Noticing his latest fans, Nigel winks at the girls and tightens his pose.

"Calm down," I say, causing Rah to chuckle. Nigel throws me a look and smiles. My boy knows he's out of line.

The girls look at me and I glare back. I could care less who they think they are. I hate it when chicks stunt a dude I'm with if they don't know our relationship status. It's just plain disrespectful.

"That's beautiful," I say, admiring the symbol drawn on the front cover of Rah's beats and rhymes notebook. "What does it mean?"

"It means vigilant warrior," Rah's says, tracing the figure with his right index finger. "It represents the horn used to call warriors to battle."

"I love it," I say, following his movement. "It reminds me of our family veve," I say, feeling the cool brass emblem against my skin. I touch my left shoulder where my flesh is still tingling from my earlier vision.

"Jayd, I think it's time you got some ink on that smooth skin of yours. And don't worry about the cost; it's on me," Nigel says, like it's as easy as that.

My dream a little while ago may have been a premonition. Mama's always saying I should pay closer attention to my dreams. Before I went to sleep I sought an answer on how to beat my great-grandfather in order to defeat Esmeralda's plan. This might be the response I was looking for. I look down at my left shoulder and examine the same spot where Califia and the other captives were burned. The heat rises in my body indicating to me that I'm on the right path.

"Funny thing is I had a dream about getting branded. I guess if I got one it would be of this," I say, pulling the charm out of my shirt and showing it to Nigel.

Mickey and Sandy are the only girls I know with tattoos. Misty wanted one back in the day but we were too young. Actually, we're still too young but Julian's a client of theirs and looks the other way when bartering for herb.

"It would be nice to see your wild side come out for a change," Rah says, touching my bare arm with the back of his hand. He still gives me the chills but the vibe isn't as strong as it once was.

I stare at my friends excited about the challenge. Am I really about to do this?

"I'm in," I say before I can chicken out. My boys aren't going to let me go back on my word.

"All right then," Julian says, stripping down the plastic covering on his now empty chair. He replaces the cover and ushers me to sit down. "Ladies first."

Nigel and Rah take a seat in one of the chairs along the wall with a clear view of the session. I can't believe I'm doing this. It feels like everything's changing: my friends, my powers, and now my body. When are things going to go back to the way they were?

"I'll take the symbol and trace it," Julian says, reaching for my eleke.

"No," I say, protecting my veve. "I'll draw it myself."

"No problem," Julian says, passing me a pen and pad.

"Hey, Jayd. You remember when me and Rah got our first tat last year?" Nigel asks, eyeing the girls as they leave the shop. He has enough chick problems as it is. "You were afraid it was going to come to life like in that one *Tales from the Crypt* episode with Heavy D."

"R.I.P. to a legend," Rah says. Heavy D was one of his favorite old school artists.

"Yeah, I do," I say, laughing at my boys. "That's not the image I need in my head at the moment, Nigel, but thanks," I say, passing my best version of the image to Julian.

"My bad, girl," Nigel says, laughing at my hesitation. "You got this."

Julian makes a copy of the image, drenches the paper in some sort of solution and places it on my left shoulder. As soon as the wet paper touches my skin my nerves calm and I feel good about my decision.

"That's it, Jayd. Deep breath in, deep breath out," Rah says like he's some sort of tattoo guru. "It feels good, doesn't it?"

"Yes, it does." The tingling sensation of the veve print gives me a surge of physical and spiritual energy I couldn't have anticipated.

"Are you ready?" Julian asks, inadvertently showcasing his tongue ring. This dude is tatted and pierced up.

"Yes, I am." I lean forward in the chair and breathe deeply, allowing Califia's stories to take over my thoughts.

The needle's initial contact with my skin is hot and prickly. I follow Rah's advice and continue my breathing exercises but can't ignore the nuisance on my shoulder.

"Relax into it, my child. It'll be over soon. Then, you'll have a beautiful symbol of your lineage to carry with you always, scaring the right people straight," Califia says into my mind. My great ancestor's presence calms my anxiety. Once I surrender to the process the buzzing sound of the tattoo gun makes me forget all about the slight pain.

"That's fresh," Nigel says, eyeing my ink but I'm too relaxed to care. I'll wait until it's all over before checking it out. I know the veve will be perfect.

"Done," Julian says, spraying my shoulder down with the same anti-bacterial solution he used to clean the spot a moment ago.

"You were out like a light," Rah says.

"Check it out." Julian passes me a hand mirror and spins the chair around. I catch my reflection in the vanity and inspect the work.

Rah takes a picture with his cell and sends it to Nigel and me.

"Wow," I say, amazed at how much it resembles Califia's brand. "It's even more beautiful than I thought it would be."

Nigel nods in agreement. I'm glad my boys were here to witness the evolution of Jayd Jackson. I wish my girls were also here.

"Glad you like it," Julian says, meeting my eyes in the mirror. "Keep it covered for a couple of hours. You can bathe, just don't wash the tat directly or put anything but antibacterial ointment on it until it's completely healed." Julian slathers *Neosporin* over the veve before wrapping it in plastic.

"How long will that take?" I ask, touching the plastic armband. Just like that, I've lost my tattoo virginity.

"A couple of weeks. After the scab's all gone you're good to go," Julian says. He cleans the area and claims a new needle package for his next canvas.

"Jayd, you can hook up my hair tomorrow," Rah says, running his fingers through his Afro. "I'll pay you double since I know you wanted to take the day off and whatnot."

"Cool," I say, glad for the night off and extra pay. Even if I wanted to I think I'm too excited to braid.

"Yeah, let's hit up *Roscoe's* after this," Nigel says, speaking my language.

They smoked a blunt before I got to Rah's house. Their munchies have arrived in full effect. I didn't even get a contact high and I could eat a number nine with a side of greens and a Lisa's Delight myself.

"Sounds like a plan, black man." I'm excited about my new step toward adulthood, or at least that's what I'm going to say when my mom and Mama find out. Hopefully they won't be too upset. It's not like when I was thirteen and got my ears pierced without their permission. That was a bad day. I never even got a chance to sport my new earrings. When Mama saw my ears she made me take them out immediately under the threat of her removing them for me.

"Now we're connected for life, Jayd. You know that, right?" Nigel says as he takes my place in the tattoo chair. "We're kinfolk, girl."

"Is that right?" I ask, eyeing myself in the mirror. All of a sudden I feel more badass than ever before.

"Yeah, girl," Rah says. I make myself comfortable in a seat next to my long-time friend and rest my head on his shoulder. "Sharing ink with somebody's like sharing blood, nahmean?" Rah tilts his head back on the glass and shuts his eyes, patiently waiting his turn.

I miss the ease Rah and I used to share. It would be nice if we could get back to that place after all of this madness our crew's experiencing blows over. I begin to drift off myself but the sight of Califia and Cortez fighting over her self-brand comes to the forefront of my mind. There's something empowering about marking your territory even if it's on your own body. I don't blame Califia for taking matters into her own hands. Unfortunately, it's also how she became an ancestor.

"That's it," I say aloud. I look around to see if anyone heard me but Rah's practically snoring and Nigel's in his tattoo vibe. From what I can tell Julian's almost done; the art looks good.

I return my head to Rah's shoulder and contemplate my revelation. I think Rousseau's trying to join our bloodline anyway he can: First, through biting one of Mama's godchildren and then again by unsuccessfully chasing me down and trying to take a bite out of my ass. After all these years he knows he can't get to Mama directly and will go through anyone—or anything—to do it. So, what's his master plan? I'll focus on Rousseau and our family business and let Mama handle G's trial. It's time Rousseau got a taste of his own medicine. If he wants a bite out of us so bad I'll make sure he gets all that he desires and more.

"Some people want nothing more than to be loved, and will go through all types of extremes to get it."
-Mama
Drama High, volume 8: Keep It Movin'

Chapter 7
DESPERATE MEASURES

So far it's been a peaceful Monday allowing me to get through most of my schoolwork uninterrupted. I even studied up on the shape shifter next door for about an hour before Rah called to remind me that I needed to braid his hair. According to the spirit book, Rousseau—in one form or another—was my great-grandfather's favorite godson and chosen apprentice. When Jon Paul died, Rousseau attempted to bring him back to life, per Jon Paul's instructions, but instead turned himself into a shape-shifter with one foot in and one foot out of the afterlife. I guess he wasn't that great of a student.

The most important thing I learned was that Jon Paul's unsettled spirit can move between the spirit and physical worlds when summoned by Rousseau. No wonder Esmeralda called on her former lover to come back into her life. With my great-grandfather's powers from beyond the grave and his highly favored servant loyal to her, Esmeralda's paving the way to become quite the formidable adversary. Esmeralda's after our lineage and there's no telling what she'll do to get a drop of a Williams woman's blood.

Nigel and Rah have already started the special Monday chill session. The loud studio speakers shake the entire house. With both Mickey and Sandy gone Rah's glad to finally have the space back to himself and so are we. Weekends at Rah's house used to be like heaven for my crew and me. It's the relief we needed after dealing with Drama High all week long. Eventhough Rah attends a different school we all know every high school has its share of drama no matter the name on the front of the building.

"I don't hustle and flow, man/I hustle my flow," Nigel says through the mic in their homemade studio booth. The fact that they converted the garage into a full-fledged work and chill space is impressive. If push comes to shove Nigel and Rah can always open a home improvement business.

"If it isn't the young queen herself," Rah says from his desk, focused on the hundreds of dials in front of him. His studio equipment cost more than my mom's car. "How's the shoulder?"

"It's okay," I say, touching the sensitive ink. "I almost forgot it was there."

I nod what's up to Chase and Alia who are into the football game on the big screen.

"That's how the addiction starts, sis," Ra
ing me a kiss me on the cheek. "Next thing
you'll be tatted up like us."

I laugh at Rah and place my hair bag down on the floor next to the coffee table covered with various CDs, magazines and books. I think I'll lie across the futon while I wait for Rah and Nigel to finish up their recording session.

"It's a verb not a noun/Don't let me see you try and clown/I'll turn that smile upside down because we takin' all fake ass niggas down."

"Nigel sounds good," I say. Rah nods in agreement.

"Slangin' is my job/spittin' is my talent/I know some of you weak ass punks can't handle it/Got the looks, got the brains/Score on average five touchdowns in a game," Nigel says vehemently into the booth microphone. He's the only one inside the enclosed space no larger than a shower but it sounds like he's performing in front of thousands of people he's so passionate. I haven't heard him rap like this in a minute.

"We takin' these streets back like soldiers in Iraq/ Street soldiers/I told ya/We're street soldiers."

"That's a wrap," Rah says, signaling Nigel to come out of the booth. How he knows one button from the next on his massive production system is beyond me.

"Y'all should see if you can get on Bryan's show," I say. Bryan would be impressed by their skills, too. "New artists battle once a month."

"I've heard them cats on there before," Rah says, removing his headphones. "We got them niggas all day, sun."

I'm not a groupie but I agree. They can hold their own with the best of them.

"Word," Nigel says, giving his boy props. "What up, girl?" Nigel walks over to where I'm relaxing and gives me a big hug.

"I need a smoke break," Chase says, rising from the floor where he was comfortably seated between Alia's knees. The game must not be going his way if he's taking a breather.

"When are you going to give up those death sticks?" I ask. I don't know what it is with people and cigarettes. If you know something is slowly poisoning you why continue doing it?

"When death comes and gets me." Chase thinks that shit is funny but Mama says we should never tempt Iku, the orisha over death. He's always on the hunt for people making transition from one life to the next whether they're ready for it or not.

"Jayd, lighten up," Alia says, taking a pack of *Newports* from her hemp purse and passing it to her man. I guess they're in the same coffin.

"You too, Alia?" I can't say that I'm completely shocked. Most of the kids at South Bay High are into some sort of drug use, legal or otherwise. "How are you going to be a vegetarian and smoke cigarettes at the same time?"

"We're not old ladies, Jayd," Alia says, taking a long, menthol cigarette out of the box. "Live a little."

Nigel smiles at me and returns to listening to the track they just recorded. I love it when my boys are in their flow. It puts us all in a good mood.

"Jayd was born old," Rah says, making himself comfortable on the floor in front of me. I guess he's ready for me to get to work.

"Shut up, fool," I say, smacking him in the back of his head. "I want to live a long life if I can help it, that's all I'm saying." My logic is falling on deaf ears. Out of my crew, Nellie and me are the only ones who don't drink or smoke.

"Jayd, can you hook a brotha up after you finish Rah's braids?" Chase asks, leading his girlfriend outside. Rah doesn't allow tobacco smoke in his house. "I've been growing out my afro," Chase says, running his fingers through his wavy brown hair.

Chase will go through any measure to put his newfound blackness on display, poor thing. His hair is getting long, but unlike Jeremy's kinky locs via his Jewish heritage, Chase's hair is curly at best. It'll take a whole lot of maneuvering to get his braids to stay in tact.

"I'll see what I can do," I say, focusing on Rah's full head of hair.

Rah passes me my hair bag—a stylist is nothing without her tools. Using my favorite red comb I part Rah's thick hair already knowing he wants ten braids straight back. He's fully relaxed and I'm into my flow. We're all enjoying the melodic beats courtesy of Nigel.

After a while, Chance and Alia make their way back inside. "Nice bag," I hear Alia say before stepping inside. Who's she talking to?

"Hey," Trish says, walking through the back door like she lives here. Really?

"What up, Trish?" Nigel says. She looks at me without so much as a blink.

Trust, the feeling's mutual.

"What up, girl?" Rah says. He nods at his ex, looks up at me and shrugs his shoulders as if to say he doesn't know what the pop-up visit's for, either.

"I got your mail," Trish says, handing the stack to Rah. She looks me in the eye and I dare her to say something smart about me braiding Rah's hair. She's not his girlfriend anymore, and even when she was her hating couldn't stop me from making my paper, tricks be damned.

"It's about time my applications got here," Rah says, claiming three large envelopes from the stack of mostly bills with his mom's name on it. Too bad Carla's constantly absent from her children's lives. Sandy probably sees her more than her own sons do since the two of them dance at the same club. Trifling doesn't even begin to describe Rah's mother. It's a wonder he's turned out as stable as he has.

"One of those had better be from UCLA," Nigel says over the music.

Nigel's parents can afford to send him anywhere he wants to go even if both his football talent and his good grades guarantee him a scholarship. It must be nice to already have your college career path on lock while the rest of us pray we get in somewhere.

Trish takes a seat at the desk making herself a little too comfortable for my taste. Doesn't she have a bitch's convention to attend with her best friend and Nigel's ex,

Tasha? Come to think of it, I don't think I've ever seen one without the other.

"I didn't know you were applying to Clark?" I say, observing the first envelope.

I know Rah's thought about moving to Atlanta for a while. He's got family out there and it'll be a good change of atmosphere. We're both too young to have as much responsibility as we do.

"Yeah, I'm thinking about it. You know I haven't seen my brother and the rest of pop's family since I was a kid," Rah says, tilting his head to left. There are only four more rows left to braid.

"I never knew you had other siblings," Trish says, out of the loop as usual. Why is she still here?

"Yeah, I do," Rah says, causing Trish's expressionless face to slightly crinkle. "Anyway, I also want to be closer to the music industry out there. Besides, it's about time Rahima got to know her grandfather, and the further we're away from Sandy the better."

"I can't argue with that," I say. I'll miss my boy but he needs to do what's best for his family.

"I know where I'm going," Trish says even though no one asked about her life plans. "To Spelman because my mom's an alumnus. It'll be so cool going to college in the same area."

Wait a minute. Trish is applying to Spelman? What the hell?

"Well isn't that convenient," I say, pulling Rah's row into place tighter than necessary. It's the last braid and I want to make sure he feels my pain.

"You should apply to the HBCU's in Atlanta, too Jayd. Georgia's a big place." Rah thinks he's slick. He can sell that shit to Chase but I don't want to leave California and he knows it. Mama would kill me for even thinking about leaving the LA area let alone moving down south.

"Whatever," Trish says, sounding as annoyed as I am. "When's my god baby coming home? I want to take her to the mall with me and Tasha."

"Oh no, Trish. I know you're tripping now," I say, spraying my lemon-coconut hair sheen over Rah's immaculate style. "I'm her godmother, not you."

Trish looks at Rah with a crooked smile spread across her beet-red lips. Rah looks up at me then down at the floor like he's guilty as sin.

"Rah, what the hell is she talking about?" I ask, the spray aimed in the air.

Trish, Nigel, Chase and Alia watch as the calm scene quickly gets live. Before Trish walked in we were chilling. Broads always bring heat wherever they go.

"Jayd, it's just on paper and there was no reason for you to know about any of it," Rah says, glaring at Trish. "It's for the courts. There has to be some relationship between Trish and Rahima other than her being my..." Rah begins but trails off in the middle of the word.

"Not saying it doesn't make it any less true, Rah. Spit it out," I say, looking at my friends. I know they only know each other through me, but I suddenly feel like I don't belong here anymore.

"We're back together, Jayd," Trish says, taking the words out of Rah's mouth. "Get a clue." Trish should've left five seconds ago when I could still see straight.

"Y'all might as well just go on and get married, make it official," Chase says, attempting to bring some levity to the situation to keep me from going off. Chase thinks he's just being funny, but I can tell by Trish's reaction she's had the same thought.

"What the hell, Rah? Are you seriously considering getting married, to her?" I feel like I'm in a Vesta video. This is not an episode of *Unsung* and I'm not about to cry over this fool. I'm way too young for this shit.

I know Rah's desperate to gain full custody of his daughter but marriage isn't the answer. Sandy's pregnant with Trish's brother's baby, the two of them are shacked up at Trish's house, and now Rah's also making Trish Rahima's godmother. This is too much ignorance to tolerate, even for the best of friends.

"Jayd, calm down," Rah says. Nothing good ever comes after those three words. I know it's time for me to go.

"Bye, y'all." I smack Rah in the back of the head as I collect my things and make a move. This is too much bull for me to deal with, especially on my day off.

"But what about my hair, Jayd?" Chase asks. "You promised you'd hook me up after Rah?" He must be kidding. Didn't he hear the same conversation we all did?

"Chase, I said I'd try. But your extra-soft hair needs a little more length for me to pull the braids into shape." I could smack the shit out of Chase right now. He's lucky his mama's helping Mama and me out. "I'll stop by your house next week and give it a shot."

"Jayd, come on, girl. We haven't even officially started the session yet," Nigel says, rolling a blunt. I wouldn't be a part of that rotation anyway.

"Jayd, it's not that serious," Trish says, sounding more like Paris Hilton than the bougie hood girl she most definitely is. "Besides, you're just his hair braider, not his woman. That's my position."

"Whatever," I say, charging out the back door with Rah at my heels. When was he going to tell me that he was dating Trish again? This is the same stunt he pulled in junior high when he started seeing Sandy behind my back. I didn't tolerate the shit then and I certainly won't now.

"Jayd, please. Talk to me," Rah says, grabbing my arm.

"Ouch," I say, pulling away from him. My tattoo begins to burn from the contact.

"I'm sorry, Jayd. You know I'd never do anything to hurt you." Rah begins to explain his stupid actions but I have no patience to hear his rationale this afternoon.

"Rah, I don't want to know what you and that girl are doing."

"Jayd, listen. In order to solidify custody of Rahima I have to prove to the courts that I can provide a stable home for her. That means no more slanging and a steady girlfriend. Now, since you'd rather live in La-La land with your white boy I've got to do what's necessary for my daughter before Sandy tries to pull another stunt."

I don't care what the reason behind it is. Rah knows this is the end of anything that could've possibly happened between us.

"I told you when you begged to be back in my life last year that if you ever lied to me about anything again that would be the last time I'd forgive you," I say, remembering our verbal contract. I should've got it in writing.

"But Jayd, this is different. This is real shit, not me cheating on you over something stupid," Rah says, now screaming at the top of his lungs.

"I don't give a damn the reason behind it, Rah," I yell, matching his octave range. "The fact is that you didn't trust me enough to tell me the truth." Tears well up in my eyes and Rah's begin to glisten as well. "You're a liar, Rah. Forget you know me."

"Jayd," Rah yells to my back and he can keep yelling for all I care. Sometimes he makes the worst decisions ever. Letting Sandy move in was one, and getting back with Trish is definitely another.

I start my mom's car, pressing hard on the clutch until it finally turns the ignition. Why did Rah have to go and screw up when my mom's car is tripping? This dude's really got my head spinning. But as Trish so eloquently stated, Rah's no longer my problem. Trish can have him and his baby mama drama. This is the last time Rah gets to make me cry.

"My main question is how do some chicks do it? And, more importantly, how can I be down?"
-Jayd
Drama High, volume 7: Hustlin'

Chapter 8
IRREPLACEABLE

So far it's been a rough week at school and we weren't even here for the first day. These freshman chicks are getting on my nerves, whispering about the black witch of South Bay High with Misty and Emilio fueling their superstitious beliefs. Now that she and KJ are officially over she's got too much time on her hands. And to add to my issues, Mrs. Bennett's been tripping hard on my weekly assignments, saying that I need to dig deeper into my subconscious to understand the complex nature of the literature in her class. I want to tell her to kiss my complex ass but I don't think that would solve the problem.

Unfortunately, Misty and Mrs. Bennett don't compare to the shade the new bitch in my life's throwing my way. Cameron's using the photo of her kissing my estranged boyfriend to gain popularity while attempting to win Jeremy over, who's absent today. With yesterday being a holiday and today being the standard short

Tuesday, I guess Jeremy didn't see the point of making an appearance. I may not like Jeremy's bad habits, but I'm not sure that I'm completely done with us yet. Even if I am, I'll be damned if he rebounds with Cameron.

"Okay class. It's good to see everyone," Mr. Adewale says. It's definitely good to see him, even if his class is mostly full of the same people I try to avoid at all cost. "We need to formally greet our new student who's transferred into the class last minute," he says, gesturing toward a sistah with the thickest hair I've ever seen sitting up front.

"Hello," she quietly says without rising. "My name is Marcia Naranjo and I'm from San Francisco."

"Welcome to Speech and Debate, Marcia," Mr. Adewale says, showcasing his dimples and bright eyes. "Okay class, please take out last week's assignment and be ready to give your rebuttals to today's posted debate topic." Mr. Adewale gestures toward the white board from the corner of his desk, his favorite seat during class.

"Mr. Adewale, I left my homework at the crib," KJ says. Only he and his followers laugh at his immaturity. Even Misty's unimpressed with his outburst.

"Well, perhaps you should ask your mommy to bring it to school for you," Emilio says, shocking every one, including Mr. Adewale.

When Emilio first transferred to South Bay from his school in Venezuela last year, Mr. Adewale was like his big brother, especially since we all share the same religion. But Emilio's changed ever since he joined Hector's spiritual house. Who knows what he's capable of now that he's under Esmeralda's influence?

"What the hell did you just say to me, fool?" KJ says, rising from his seat in the back of the classroom. "You need to learn to mind your own business before your Mexican mouth writes some checks your punk ass can't cash."

"I'm from Venezuela, not Mexico," Emilio says, coolly. "You should get a map, too when you retrieve your homework." Emilio smiles at Misty who's seated next to him, much like he did when I intervened between KJ and Misty last week to keep her from getting pimp slapped and him from going to jail.

Misty returns the smile, her blue contacts aglow. What the hell?

KJ charges toward Emilio's seat. Quickly, Mr. Adewale jumps to his feet and in two steps stops KJ's fatal advance.

"Okay, you two," Mr. Adewale says, calming the situation. "That's enough. KJ, return to your seat and we'll talk about your missed assignment later."

KJ reluctantly sits down with his eyes focused on Emilio. Emilio winks at Misty and shrugs the confrontation off. I, on the other hand, am very worried about what their end goal is.

"We have our first competition of the year in two weeks at St. Agatha's Catholic School in Westwood, directly across from the UCLA campus. I expect all Forensic club members to sign up." Damn, that means me.

Reid and Laura almost look giddy at the announcement, and so does Cameron. Shit. The last thing I need is something else to do, but like my counterparts, I need just as many extracurricular points on my college applications as they do.

"Hey, Jayd," Chase says, whispering into my ear from the seat behind me. Nellie, Mickey and Nigel are seated across the room pretending to listen but the announcements don't concern them. The only club they're apart of is the African Student Union. "There's a party after school at Matt's house. You should stop by. It'll take your mind off of Rah and his bull." Chase is right. I haven't forgiven him for his flippant attitude toward yesterday's news. A break from the norm is definitely in order.

"Maybe I can come through for a minute." With Mama and Netta taking their Tuesday at the shop to spend at the jail with G and his attorney, I could actually stay for a while.

Mama keeps trying to emphasize a murder trial isn't a game but G couldn't give a damn. They've been dedicated to helping him even if he seems hell-bent on sabotaging his case. It's almost as if he has a get-out-of-jail card he's going to pop out at any second.

"Let's get started on those arguments," Mr. Adewale says.

If it's one thing I'm tired of it's fighting with folks. At least in class my venting will be productive, not that I really care about our mock topic. Between a good debate and eating the expensive spread Matt's sure to provide later, perhaps this day will end on a good note after all.

Mr. Adewale threw me for a loop earlier with the competition announcement. How am I supposed to prepare for a debate a couple of weeks from now, run membership recruitment for our club by homecoming in three weeks, and work all at the same time? I swear, if there was a spell to split me in two I'd whip it up in a hot minute. People like Matt can hire others to help him out when needed, like all of the servers running around his house party. It looks like Buckingham Palace in here rather than an afterschool get-together. His parties are always off the chain—one of the many perks of being a member of the Drama Club.

"I didn't expect to see you here, Jayd," Alia says, giving me a huge hug with her vodka breath and all. "This is Marcia. She just started today."

I guess Alia forgot we are in several of the same classes all day long. Marcia's not on the Advanced Placement track but we do share both of Mr. Adewale's classes.

"Hey, Marcia. It's nice to officially meet you," I say, greeting the new chick on the block.

"Hey, Jayd. It's nice to meet you, too," Marcia says, barely audible over the loud music and people surrounding us.

She looks like she's mixed with black and something else, but we'll have the official ASU recruitment chat later. Right now I'm only interested in the chicken wings I smell coming from the bar area.

"I don't mean to be rude but I'm starving," I say, eyeing the plates full of food circling the room. I want to make a b-line to the buffet without seeming desperate. Times have been tough. Eating anything outside of the three basic daily meals is a luxury I can't afford to pass up.

"Let's get you fed then, shall we?" Alia says with enough joy to go around. I shake my head at my inebriated homegirl as she leads the way toward the food area.

"Is she always like this?" Marcia asks, following us to the edge of the majestic basement.

Matt's parents recently remodeled the entire lower floor of the three-story house—inside and out. The garage is now considered an extension of the pool house with the basement left strictly for entertaining.

"There's my girl," Chase says, holding up a glass or brown liquor, his favorite. "Hey Jeremy, look who I found?"

Chase steps aside to reveal Jeremy sitting on a stool at the bar. Chase thinks he's funny setting me up like this—I'll have words with him after I eat.

"You should never piss off your hairdresser," I say, whispering into his ear while giving him a quick hug before Alia claims him. I don't know what it is about Chase but he seems to attract some clingy females. First Nellie, now Alia.

"That's right," Chase says, running his fingers through his head of loose curls. "You're supposed to be hooking my braids up. I'm gonna look flyy, right babe?"

Alia nods in agreement and makes herself comfortable in Chase's arms. Marcia stands next to them and eyes the rest of the crowded room. My eyes are fixated on Jeremy and his on me.

"Jayd," Jeremy says, pulling me into a hug. Damn, he smells good enough to eat. Why does he always have to smell so fresh and clean? Maybe if he stunk I'd be less attracted to him.

"What's up Paul Walker, Gabrielle Union," Seth says, laughing at his own humor.

I don't know why drunk, white boys always think racial jokes are funny no matter how inappropriate.

"Let me guess, Seth," Jeremy says, snacking on a chicken wing. "You caught up on your fantasy fiction this weekend, right?" Jeremy says, walking past Seth and out onto the back deck where the party's really poppin'.

Seth rolls his heavily lined eyes at Jeremy and wisely chooses to let the comment ride. He knows better than to push Jeremy too far.

Chance and Alia follow Jeremy outside with Marcia in tow. I fill up my plate and then follow them outside—a full mouth will keep me from the saying the wrong thing to Seth and any other haters I may encounter this afternoon.

"What happened to you two?" Seth asks, not taking the hint that we don't want to be followed. "You were such a happy couple. Now all the doom and gloom."

Jeremy posts up against the side of the wooden deck while the rest of us take a seat on the adjacent long bench. "How do you know we're not still the happy couple?" Jeremy asks with a stern look.

"Are you?" Marcia asks. She's all up in the mix and it's only her first day. Somebody better school this girl on how things work around here and quick before she's too bold around the wrong person.

"It's complicated," I say, answering for Jeremy and me. I look up at my friend, my estranged man, my confidante, and search for some sort of resolution in his eyes. All I see is a mirror filled with pain staring back at me.

"Is it really?" Chase asks. I know he's not adding heat to the flames. "Either you're together or not. Which is it?"

Jeremy and I continue looking at each other, both wanting to say something but stopping short of giving a solid answer. I guess we're both afraid to say it aloud for fear that it will become real: Is this the end of us?

"I need a drink," Jeremy says. That might not be what I wanted to hear but it may be just the answer I needed.

I return my focus to the plate on my lap ready to devour the comfort food.

"Hey, Jayd," Nellie says, walking outside through the opened patio doors. "I didn't know you'd be here."

"That makes two of us," I say, unapologetically licking the hot sauce from my fingers. "What are you doing here?" What I meant to say was what everyone else around me is thinking: You're not with Chase anymore, which means you're no longer affiliated with the Drama Club, so what the hell are you doing at one of our functions?

"Oh, Laura invited me," she says, gesturing toward Laura, Cameron and the rest of their bitch crew on the back lawn. "Didn't I tell you they're supporting me for Senior Homecoming princess this year? I'm so excited!" Nellie says, about to burst out of her body-hugging *Bebe* outfit. "I might be the first black queen at South Bay High. I can't wait to make history not once but twice."

Great, that's just what we need. Nellie's head got so large after last year's victory it took everything in me not to slap her on several different occasions.

"Kind of like Jayne Kennedy did back in the day," Marcia says, again adding her voice unnecessarily. I don't mind her outspokenness; it's actually kind of refreshing. But everyone's not going to share my view.

Nellie looks at the new girl on deck like she's a leper but chooses to ignore her comment for the time being.

"That woman was official back in the day," Chase says, nodding his head in recognition of the first black woman to grace the cover of *Playboy* magazine, or any magazine for that matter.

Seth looks at Chase like he's speaking Dutch. "Is that one of the Kennedy's, like the former Governor's wife?" Seth asks. I'm surprised he knows that much.

"No, dude. Not at all," Jeremy says, laughing at Seth.

"I'm surprised you don't know who she is, man," Chase says. Alia looks as clueless as Seth does. She also looks jealous at Chase's obvious crush on yet another sistah much to Nellie's liking. "Jayne Kennedy was one of the baddest divas that ever graced the cover of a magazine and made history while doing it."

Seth's eyes brighten at the thought of another bold and beautiful woman to look up to. Everyone's well aware that Seth is gay, happy and proud about it. He's in charge of make up and wardrobe for the Drama Club as well as the set designs for our shows. He takes pride in his work and in being the nosiest gossip at South Bay High.

"Hello all," Cameron says, stepping onto the deck leaving the rest of her rich, mean girl crew on the lawn to soak up some sun. I hope they sizzle and burn.

"Mmmm," Alia says, under her breath. She must be drunk acting out like this. She never has anything negative to say unspoken or otherwise.

"Cameron," Jeremy says, taking a sip of his spiked iced tea courtesy of the servers on deck. I hope he's been thinking about heeding my words per our last conversation. All that alcohol and smoking is liable to get him in trouble again. If it weren't for his bad habits we wouldn't be in this mess.

"Let's check out the deejay," Chase says, taking his girlfriend by the hand and heading toward the other side of the pool.

"Love the new shades, Nellie," Cameron says. "*Gazelles*?"

"Yeah, thanks," Nellie says, removing the expensive sunglasses. "They were a gift." There's something about her tone that makes me think that compliment was code for something else.

"I'll come with," Marcia says, sensing the thick vibe. At least she has that much sense.

Seth looks at Cameron and Jeremy, then down at me taking the hint as well. Damn, this broad can clear a crowd—true evil tends to possess that divine ability.

Nellie stays put but looks anxious as hell. I'll see what that's all about later. Just a moment ago she was on cloud nine envisioning yet another crown on her already swollen head. Our crew barely made it through her last coronation, now we may possibly have another one on its way. I don't know if we can go through that again.

"Jeremy, I'm glad I ran into you," Cameron says, attempting to loop her arm through his. Jeremy moves before she can make contact.

"Why is that?" Jeremy asks, impatient by his neighbor's giddy demeanor.

I continue polishing off my plate ready for seconds. Even this wench can't ruin my appetite.

"I wanted to discuss our Homecoming plans, silly," Cameron says.

"We don't have any plans, Cameron," Jeremy says without attempting to hide his disgust for the trick. At least we can agree on something.

Would it be too crude of me to accidentally toss my drink in her face?

"Of course we do, Jeremy," Cameron says, taking the drink out of his hand and sipping on it. "You'll be escorting me to all of the Homecoming festivities in a few weeks." She attempts to take another sip but Jeremy reclaims his drink before she can get too comfortable with it. "And since it's our senior year let's make the occasion yearbook worthy, shall we? We should really shop for our outfits this weekend. We don't want to wait until the very last moment. Wouldn't you agree, Nellie?"

Nellie looks from me to Cameron waiting from me to spill my drink all over this trick, but Jeremy intervenes before I can go off.

"Cameron, I'm not going anywhere with you. No matter what you and my mom may think we're not dating and we never will."

Nellie looks at Cameron afraid to move a muscle. I swear she knew this was coming but how?

"That's where you're wrong, Jeremy," Cameron says, taking out her cell phone and displaying the planted picture like it's a newborn child. "According to this photo, we're not only dating but we're loving every minute of it. And happy couples do things together like attend social functions, which you will be doing a lot of this year so get used to it."

"Cameron, what the hell have you been smoking?" I ask, tired of her rant.

"And can I have some because that shit's got you high as a satellite," Jeremy says, making me laugh. I've missed his sense of humor.

Cameron shoots Jeremy a look that brings her serious tone right back to the forefront. The last time Jeremy almost went to jail for selling weed on campus I made him a batch of cupcakes to get him out of that legal mess. His father's attorneys also came in handy, but it really could have gone either way. They warned Jeremy then that if he got into trouble again the judge would have no problem throwing him in jail no matter how much clout his parents may have. Cameron knows she's got Jeremy right where she wants him—away from me and into her prom pictures.

"Let's just cut to the chase, shall we?" Cameron says, studying the photo. "If you deny that we were making out like we couldn't keep our hands off of each other you'll have to admit that you were high in the picture." Cameron's really tripping, so much so that she's almost gangster with her shit, inspiring a little fear in me that she might actually get away with this stunt.

I know Jeremy doesn't want to miss his senior year for anything, most of all jail time. By drinking and smoking weed he'd be in violation of his parole agreement and on his way back to court.

"Cameron, are you that hard up for a man that you'll blackmail one who quite obviously wants nothing to do with you into dating you? Really?" I ask, amazed at how vengeful a wench can be.

"Don't worry about my motivations, Jayd. As of this moment, Jeremy Edward Weiner is no longer your concern. TTYL, babe." Cameron smiles wickedly, blows a kiss to Jeremy and walks away.

Nellie looks after her mentor like she wants to follow but hesitates. What the hell?

"I'm going to tell my attorney about Cameron staging the photo and blackmailing me and see if there's anything we can do," Jeremy says, visibly upset. "She's really lost her mind."

"Sanity's a crap shoot when you're in love." I say, ready to roll.

This isn't the stress-free afternoon I'd hoped for. At least I'll get some free groceries to go. There's enough food inside to feed an army and Matt always insists we take food to go. A couple of plates should last me a day or two until I can get to the market. Constantly rising gas prices are forcing us broke folks to make some tough choices these days.

I look at Nellie who looks away guilt-ridden. I'll lay into her ass over the phone or at another time. The last thing I want to do is be a part of another scene. I wipe my hands on the thick napkin and head for the patio doors.

Jeremy stops me in my tracks and blocks me from entering the doorway. "I'll do whatever it takes to get you back, Jayd."

Jeremy walks through the door ahead of me and vanishes inside the spacious basement, no doubt to find a bong and smoke his brains out in an attempt to forget about Cameron's latest revelation. I can't even enjoy my last jumbo shrimp. I don't know if it bothers me more that Jeremy allowed himself to get into this situation or that Cameron's got him right where she wants him and how that affects me.

"Is everything okay?" Chase asks, stepping behind me and rubbing my shoulders.

Nellie looks pissed but can't say shit about who Chase chooses to touch. She lost that right when she gave up on him—one of the biggest mistakes she's ever made since I've known her. I know she could kick herself now that Alia's snagged her ex-boo up.

"Not at all. I wish I knew who sent me that picture," I say, thinking out loud. "Then I might be able to help Jeremy check Cameron without getting in trouble for it. I know there's some sort of law against what she did."

Nellie replaces the shades over her eyes and looks around anxiously like she stole something. What the hell is wrong with her?

"That's actually not a bad idea, depending on who sent the picture and if they're willing to testify against Cameron. Good luck with that," Chase says, sympathetically tapping me on the shoulder.

Chance knows as well as I do that Cameron's replaced Jeremy's baby-mama, Tania as the head bitch in charge. Sometimes I wish Jeremy weren't the most wanted dude at South Bay High. Then there wouldn't be so many hating females to deal with on the regular.

Nellie shifts from one butt cheek to the other like her shorts are on fire. She then removes her glasses again and looks sadly at Chase.

"Nellie, are you okay?" I ask. "The bathroom's inside if you need to go," I say, gesturing toward the patio doors.

She looks down at her uneaten veggie platter and plays with her celery sticks. "Jayd, I sent you the picture," Nellie says with tears in her heavily made-up eyes. "I didn't want too but Cameron was showing it off to everyone at Laura's house like she'd won some sort of bet or something. I just wanted you to know what was up."

"Nellie, say it ain't so," Chase says, disappointed in his ex girlfriend's admission.

"Damn it, Nellie! Why didn't you say something before?" I ask, pissed as all get-out.

"I wanted to but I was trapped," Nellie says, taking her napkin and dabbing her wet eyes without smearing her mascara. "If Cameron found out that I sent it from her phone I would have been seen as a traitor. Besides, I just wanted you to get the information. What difference does it matter how you got it? The most important thing is that Chase proved it was altered slightly to her advantage and now you can help Jeremy and move on, right?"

"Wrong," I say, too upset to argue with my friend. I step inside and take a deep breath.

Nellie's done some stupid shit in her day but this tops them all. How could she watch my boyfriend and I suffer at the hands of the very bitch she wants so desperately to be friends with? Loyalty means absolutely nothing to Nellie when she has her eyes set on a goal. I haven't been this mad at anyone for a long time and to make it worse, I don't know who I'm more angry with: Jeremy, Nellie or Cameron. Why does love have to hurt every single time I find myself in the middle of it?

No one had better say another thing to me while I make my plates and escape this scene. If the wrong person steps up I'm liable to go off and that'll only do more harm than good.

"Evil! All of you, just no good hussies."
-Church Lady
Drama High, volume 11: Cold As Ice

Chapter 9
LETHAL WEAPON

The past few days have been a blur to me and not just because I've been on my grind. Rather than face Jeremy, Cameron, Nellie or Misty and risk a fight, I've chosen to immerse myself in my schoolwork and my spirit studies much to my grandmother's delight. Mama and Netta even eased up on asking me to join them at the county jail with the other supporters, which has given me more time to think about my next moves.

So far the only decision I've made about anything is that the African Student Union needs to branch out if it's going to be a viable club. Half of the members have dropped out and the numbers continue to decline. I decided to reach out to El Barrio for new members and a few of them were happy to sign up, including Maggie. Besides, it'll be nice to hang out with her more often. Out of all of my school associates, Maggie's the most consistent with her swag making her a perfect new member.

Every time I close my eyes the picture of Jeremy and Cameron's infamous kiss comes to the front of my mind. Why did Nellie have to send me that photo? I hate it when I get jealous. It's such a dangerous and useless emotion, but that's what I'm feeling. As Newton said, every action has an equal and opposite reaction, and I need to be careful when making my next move. The odu I read last night about Oshune being madly in love with Shango and tricking his first wife, Oba into cutting her ear off and putting it into his soup showed me that for sure. Like the veve on my shoulder represents, we can choose any direction we want to go in according to our heart's truest desires. Possessing a cool head when making the choice is the challenge.

Violence is not becoming of Oshune and the daughters in her lineage have paid for her jealous actions ever since. Like Oshune, when my head gets hot I can make foolish mistakes with serious repercussions. My tongue can be a lethal weapon at times and Nellie's the first target on my list.

"Jayd, what are you doing sleeping in the middle of the afternoon?" my mom asks, opening the front door. "Your aunties are going to be here any minute to help me plan for the wedding festivities. I need you to have this place spotless by then." My mom gathers my bedding off of the couch, balls it up and tosses it into the already stuffed living room closet.

"Yes, ma'am," I say, reluctantly rising from the couch. So much for taking a quick nap before getting my study on later this evening.

I was looking forward to a Saturday night chilling by myself. If I had my own room it wouldn't be such an issue, but I know that's not happening anytime soon. My mom and Karl will probably move to his apartment when they get married this summer and I'll be in a dorm room somewhere unless I get my own place. Just the thought of being completely responsible for an apartment gives me a headache.

"Why so glum, chum?" My mom used to say that to me all the time when I was a little girl. If only things could be that simple again.

"Dudes, chicks, money—you name it, I'm dealing with it," I say, watching my mom switch from one expensive pair of shoes into another perfectly complimenting her nude, strapless jumpsuit.

I wish I had the wardrobe and the girlfriends my mom has. She's been friends with the same four women since junior high school. Mama says that was the only blessing that came from her eldest daughter losing her powers—she could maintain her friendships with women from all walks of life without inciting fear in any of her true friends. All of my aunties, as I've called them since I can remember, know my mom's story and love her just the same. I'd love to have those kinds of homegirls. Instead, I've got Nellie and Mickey's selfish asses to deal with.

"Uh oh," my mom says. She passes me the glass cleaner and a roll of paper towels from the dining room table where I've left my hair mess from last night and today's appointments. My mom looks less than thrilled with my negligence but is sympathetic with my mood. "What happened now?"

"The top three?" I ask, cleaning. "Cameron's blackmailing Jeremy into being her call boy, Nellie can keep it from happening by telling the truth and having my back but she won't, and Rah's back with Trish."

"Rah's what?" my mom asks, nearly shrieking she's so shocked. "What the hell is that boy thinking?"

My mom doesn't really concern herself with my school friends but she's known Rah since we were twelve-years old. Much like the rest of my family she'll always give him the benefit of the doubt no matter what.

"Rah chose Trish—again," I say, wiping the coffee table harder than necessary. I'll be able to see through it to the apartment downstairs if I keep this up. "I don't know why I'm surprised. Dudes never pick girls like me. I'm too strong, independent, blah, blah, blah. Mean frail bitches are the only ones who win."

"Watch your mouth, little girl," my mom says.

I rarely slip up like that. I really need to take a cleansing bath like the one I read about last night. I don't have all of the ingredients nor can I imagine driving back to Compton this evening. It'll have to wait but not for too long—my head can't take much more heat.

"Mom, I'm sorry about the language and for not straightening up after my last client," I say, moving into the dining room. I always clean up right after I'm done but all I wanted to do an hour ago was pull the covers over my head and sleep. "You know I'm doing my best to keep the place clean. It seems like people are losing a lot more hair these days than they used to." One girl alone left enough hair for me to make a track out of.

"Jayd, it's not just the hair on the floor. The water and electric bills have also been very high lately. I'm not spending much time here anymore and it's honestly getting to be a drain."

"I know, mom. I'll chip in some more for the utilities." It already feels like I have my own place with the way my mom leaves me here by myself every night. I buy my own groceries and pay a small portion of the bills. All that's left is for me to pay is rent and I'll be official.

"All right, girl. But I think you should consider going to cosmetology school for your license so you can work full time in a shop." My mom's mentioned this plan before as if she doesn't know who her own mother is.

"You know Mama would never allow me to work anywhere besides Netta's shop. She'd have your head on a platter for suggesting it and I couldn't live with your death on my conscience."

My mom playfully hits me with her dust rag as I wipe the chairs free of hair, dandruff and other particles. It would be nice to have my own shop one day.

"No one's saying you should leave Netta's shop—never that," my mom says, her bright green eyes glistening as she looks around half expecting Mama to appear. "But we all have to think about your best interest, and leaving your clients on this side of town is definitely not a good idea."

"No, it's not on so many levels," I say, thinking about the sister's head I hooked up this afternoon.

I could tell she's worn extensions all of her life. Her hair was so stressed out it almost made me cry just touching it, not to mention the fact that she fell asleep while I braided her natural hair. I love what I do and I especially love it when new clients feel the difference between how I do hair and the rest of these so-called stylists out here. A lot of them could care less about their client's needs and will use anything in their hair. Mama and Netta taught me better than that.

"You should seriously consider it, Jayd," my mom says, glancing at my hair tools spread across the dining room table. "What's wrong with seeking out a license? Besides, that way you might even be able to become a partner in Netta and Mama's shop one of these days if they let you."

"Yeah, right." I sweep up the last of the synthetic hair from the kitchen floor before vacuuming the dining room carpet. I know that'll never happen.

"I'm serious, Jayd. Set yourself up for success, baby and accept nothing less. If you present yourself as a formidable candidate I'm sure Mama and Netta will happily take you seriously."

"Mama doesn't want me doing anything but focusing on my spirit work; school, hair and friends be damned."

"I know it seems like that at the moment, Jayd but Mama's only got your best interests at heart. Just prove to her that you can do it all and she'll have no choice but to let you do just that." My mom checks her reflection in the mirror above the dining room table one more time before her friends arrive.

"I'll take your word for it," I say, starting the vacuum cleaner.

"They're here, Jayd," my mom yells over the loud noise.

I quickly finish my last task satisfied with my work. I'll give the place a thorough cleaning another day. I can tell by the brown bags in my aunties' hands that they're ready to get their party on.

"Girls, we better be careful," my Aunt Frankie says, loudly leading the pack. "You know Lynn Marie probably got her man hidden in the closet somewhere."

"We ain't seen her in so long they're probably joined at the hip by now," Shannon says, the oldest and wealthiest of the crew. "We can't have him coming to the strip club with us tonight. I've got a purse full of singles and intend on spending them all." She married well, even if her husband's older than she'd like him to be. Hanging out with her friends is her only release.

"Turn around and let me see if he's in her back pocket," my Aunt Vivica says. She's my mom's best friend and matron of honor. My Aunt Anne—Mama's youngest daughter and Jay's mother—will probably be the maid of honor. I haven't heard my mom talk about it but I know that's what she's hoping for.

"After her lunch rendezvous last week I think we all need to spray some holy water in this space," my Aunt Paulette says, closing the door behind her. She's carrying a large bag of food from my favorite Chinese restaurant in downtown LA where they all work. My mom's the only one who left the company they all worked at a few years ago for a change of pace.

"What are you talking about? My mom never comes home for lunch," I say, walking over to give them each a hug.

"You don't know what I do when you're not here," my mom says, bringing all sorts of unwanted visuals to mind. "This is still my place and I'm grown, in case you forgot."

My mom pats me on the hip and heads toward the dining room to move the chairs into the living room so they can all relax. That's my cue to get out so they can be as grown as they want without me eavesdropping like I usually do. I learned how to cuss, what an orgasm was, and how to use a tampon from their conversations.

My Aunt Frankie's smoke is killing me and she just lit the first cigarette of a train to come. I'd be better off chilling at the coffee house. Hopefully Keenan is working tonight and I can explain why I've been avoiding him since our kiss a couple of weeks ago. The last thing I want to do is unload my high school bull onto him but he needs to know why I can't entertain getting involved with him.

"Jayd, is that a tattoo on your arm?" my Aunt Shannon asks, pulling my shirtsleeve down to get a closer look. That's the last time I'll give her a hug.

"Looks like fresh ink to me, scab and all," my aunt Frankie says, puffing on her long, brown cigarette. I can't believe my own aunties are busting me. Now ain't this some shit?

"Tattoo," my mom says, carrying two chairs. "Who got a new one?" My Aunt Paulette takes one chair and

Shannon the other. Vivica and Frankie sit on the couch across from them.

"Your daughter," my Aunt Paulette says, puffing on her own cigarette. My Aunt Vivica looks at her best friends and laughs at my unnecessary trial. I knew I should've escaped when I had the chance.

"Jayd, when did you get a tattoo? And where?" my mom asks, walking over to where I'm standing. "Come on, let me see it."

I'm not ashamed. Why should I be afraid of the consequences? It's not like I got my boyfriend's name tatted on my neck. That would deserve a beat down, but not this.

"It's our family veve, a spiritual tattoo representing the Williams' women lineage." I turn around and reveal my art for them to see.

My aunts stand to get a closer look. I'm falling more in love with it each day. I also can't help thinking about Rah every time I look at it.

"I think it's pretty, but you know Mama's going to have a fit when she sees what you did."

"I know," I say, looking down at my red heart with a cross through it. I touch the charm on my neck and pray for protection from Mama's impending wrath. I hope she understands why I did it. "If a broken heart isn't permanent I don't know what is."

"Oh Lawd, Lynn Marie," My Aunt Vivica says, reclaiming her seat on the edge of the couch. "Where's the wine. I can't handle this heavy teenager shit tonight."

My mom and aunts burst into laughter officially beginning their girl's night out.

"Bye, y'all," I say, laughing at my crazy aunts and mother. I need to take a quick shower and get dressed for my solo night out on the town.

It must be nice to have friends who have your back no matter what life brings your way. I've tried to be the best friend I know how to all of my friends. How is it possible to have so many people I'm responsible to yet be so lonely at the same time?

"Why aren't you worth it?"
-Jeremy
Drama High, volume 2: Second Chance

Chapter 10
YOU GOT ME

When I finally made my escape, my mom and aunts were well into the wedding planning, the many-parties before-the-wedding planning, and which strip club to frequent after all of the planning's over. As long as they're out of the apartment when I get back later so that I can get some much-needed sleep I'm good. All this friend and boy stress has been hard on my dream world and that's never healthy.

Keenan's nowhere to be found yet and I can't say that I'm surprised. He's a hot, popular athlete and he's single—Saturday nights are his for the taking. Without him here there's no one to flirt with. Lucky for me I have a ton of studying to keep me busy. I can't believe that I forgot my headphones. As a result I'm forced to listen to the hipster jazz music floating through the speakers. Every now and then some Whitney Houston or Mariah Carey might slip through, but usually it's just the standard coffee shop music. I need my playlist to get into my study flow. Otherwise I'm not only subject to the manager's pick but also to the random conversations of others around me, which can be very distracting.

"Excuse me, dear," an elderly white lady says to me from a neighboring table. Her frail touch makes me jump slightly almost like when I first saw Pam's ashen skin in my dreams.

"Yes?" I ask. Other than Keenan no one's ever spoken to me in the coffee shop before.

"Your glasses are so pretty. Where'd you get them?" she asks, making me smile.

A compliment on the specs I resent so much was the last thing I expected to hear from her. My dad forced me to go to the eye doctor, accusing me of wasting his insurance if I didn't use it and I came out with a prescription. Who knew I needed help seeing?

"The optometrist in the mall," I say, showing her the case with the information on it. "Here's the number."

"Oh, dear. I haven't been to a mall in ages, but they look so nice on you." She smiles at me displaying a row of yellow teeth from years of smoking cigarettes and drinking coffee I assume. The huge diamond rock on her ring finger says she's not hurting for cash, so why not spring for a teeth-whitening session?

"Thank you," I say, leaving her to her book and me to my stack of work.

"Making new friends, I see," Keenan says, much to my surprise. I don't need glasses to see his fine ass light up the dimly lit café.

"Hey," I say, accepting his peck on my right cheek. "I didn't think you were working tonight." But I'm so glad that he is. Keenan's soft blend of cologne and dark roast coffee makes me forget all about my issues and responsibilities.

"Where else would I be?" Where else, indeed. "I'm on my last break. I get off in a couple of hours."

"Oh, I see," I say, tapping my fingers on the work piled up in front of me.

"You look like you're making your way through that notebook of yours pretty quickly," he says, noticing my iyawo journal. I've caught up on my entries this week.

"Thank you, much. If I could just get through my senior year as victoriously I'd be the happiest black girl in LA." The stack of school essays and other assignments towers over my spirit work, as usual. If Mama had her way it would be the complete opposite.

"What colleges are you applying to?" Keenan asks. He places his leather backpack down on the floor and takes the seat across from mine. "I hope UCLA's on your list."

I don't think I could handle it if we ended up attending the same school. I'm nearly sprung on him as it is and we only see each other once a week.

"I'm not sure yet. There's this program at my homegirl's church that pays for your college applications as long as you attend the meetings, and five out of the ten colleges have to be HBCUs."

"Sounds like a good opportunity, but you know black colleges don't pay."

"So I've heard, which means I can't go." Not to mention that Mama would have a conniption fit if I went to school out of state.

I know she's secretly praying that I attend Cal State Dominguez or Long Beach State—both schools within minutes of her house. Personally, I'm planning to apply to the University of California, San Diego and San Diego State, which happens to be Jeremy's first choice of schools, too.

"Don't give up so easily," Keenan says, leaning his fine self back in the wooden chair and crossing his muscular arms across his chest. If *The Game* had a college version of the show he'd definitely be a cast member.

"Oh, I'm not. As a matter of fact I have a scholarship fund already set up from the cotillion I participated in last month, if my benefactor doesn't succeed in getting her sorority to revoke it." I won't tell him that the woman happens to be the mother of his team's top high school recruit.

"Why would she do that?" Keenan asks. How many times have I asked myself the exact same question?

"Because I embarrassed her by leaving the dance early due to an unforeseen illness," I say, recalling my hot head that night. "I'm fighting it, though. She didn't even tell me I won the damned thing."

"You know you can get that money put into a trust if you have a bank account set up in your name," Keenan says. "As long as you attend an approved school she can't touch it."

"Word?" I didn't even think about that. I bet Mrs. Esop didn't think I'd ever find out about that option, either.

"Fo shizzle," he says. I love it that Keenan and I can switch our conversation from smart to hood in an instant. It's a skill few successfully acquire. "If you bring your laptop I can show you how to download the link and get started with online banking."

This brotha's on his game and then some.

"That's cute," I say, shifting from my left butt cheek to my right. I've been sitting in the same place for over an hour and my ass is falling asleep. Too bad, because I have at least another two hours worth of work to do. As packed as the café is, Keenan looks like he's got plenty of work cut out for him this evening, too.

I wish I could live in Jeremy's world for a day. It must be nice knowing his future's secured because of his parent's wealth and connections. Chase could have the same future but he's chosen to apply to a historically black college or university, much to his mother's horror—not because she doesn't want him to attend a black college, but because she doesn't want her only child leaving home.

"Did I say something funny?" Keenan's sincere in his offer to help but he has to know that I can't afford a computer of my own.

"Everyone's not as blessed as you are, Mr. Cosby," I say, making him laugh. From what he's told me about his family the reference sounds about right.

"Do you know how much I paid for my MacBook?" Keenan asks, pulling the sleek, silver computer out of his bag.

"At least two grand," I say, admiring his notebook. "I've been to the Mac store and daydreamed."

Chase has an iPhone, an iPad and probably a few more i-contraptions I know nothing about. Most of the students at South Bay are just like him. Nigel's the only one in our crew with a computer at his parent's house but since he's not there anymore, he and Rah share the PC they mix beats on. They also let me write on it when need be if I don't get my computer work done in the library.

"Try two hundred." He places the MacBook on our shared table, smiling at my surprise.

"I never took you for the type who buys his electronics off the back of a truck in a dark alley downtown," I say, gently touching the computer. I wish I could take it home. When I get my hands on some extra money the first thing I'm going to do is hook myself up with one of these.

"Girl, I know you know better than that. I'm trying to hip you to game." Keenan types in a web address and moves his chair closer to mine so we can share the screen.

He needs to scoot back over before it gets too hot in here, and it's already pretty warm from where I'm seated.

"Why are you all up in my space?" I ask, catching another whiff of whatever else he's wearing besides coffee grounds.

"You don't mind, do you?" he says, making me blush. He's too sure of himself for me to make a smart-ass comeback quickly. "This site's for students across the country. They sell refurbished computers at a fraction of the original costs. Check it out."

Keenan expertly surfs through the site looking at the latest online deals. There are thousands of computers in all makes and models.

"You're just full of useful information, aren't you?" I ask, scanning the page.

Keenan looks up from the screen and into my eyes, making my heartbeat faster with each blink.

"I can be if you let me." Neither one of us has addressed the huge elephant in the room. The kiss was good—very good, and that's the problem.

"Keenan, I'm sorry I didn't call you after my mom walked in on our hair session," I begin. Keenan touches my hand, silencing my apology.

"Jayd, it's okay. I'm glad you came by tonight. As a matter of fact, I'd like to treat you to a late night dinner if you let me."

"Keenan, I'd love to but honestly my life is so complicated that I can't even imagine beginning anything new."

Before I can give any more excuses, Keenan squeezes my hand.

"Dinner, Jayd. That's all I'm asking," Keenan says, standing up. I guess his break's over. "I'll even let you use my laptop while I finish my shift."

The compact computer is just as tempting as its owner's offer and just in time, too. The leftovers from Tuesday's festivities ran out two nights ago and I'm tired of eating noodles.

"I could always go for a good meal," I say, running my fingers across the smooth keyboard. I bet I can type a hundred words a minute on this thing.

"Good, then it's settled. You can email yourself the documents you create so you don't have to worry about saving them on a flash."

I do have a free email account that I rarely use. I never thought of using it as a mobile flash drive.

"Another good idea," I say, opening a new document. This is going to make my schoolwork so much easier. "Have I told you how grateful I am that we met?"

"No, but you can repeatedly remind me over dinner," Keenan says, lifting my hand from the invisible mouse pad and kissing my knuckles. "Be good."

I don't know if being good is an option around this brotha. Keenan makes me excited in a way I've never felt before all while opening my eyes to new possibilities. Maybe Keenan's just the distraction I need to calm my energy so I can move forward and let go of the negativity holding me back. Perhaps being good is being with him.

It's almost midnight and the nightlife off of Wilshire Boulevard is just beginning. I didn't even know this area existed nor can I believe I'm out on a nice date with Keenan. I should be down for the count but my complimentary cappuccino has me hyped up for another round.

"Here we are," Keenan says, pulling into the parking lot of a quaint restaurant. It looks like the kind of place where famous people go to escape the limelight. "They've got the best seafood this side of town."

Keenan parks his Jeep Wrangler, exits and walks around to open my door.

"Are you sure you chose the right spot? I'm Jayd, Jayd Jackson. The high school student who would've been happy with the buffet at one of the various Ethiopian restaurants near the coffee house," I say as Keenan leads me inside.

"Not tonight, Miss Jackson."

The usher leads us to an empty booth at the front of the restaurant. "I took the liberty of ordering ahead because I haven't eaten a full meal in hours and I'm starved. I hope you don't mind."

"Not at all," I say, eyeing the expensive menu. "I wouldn't know what to order anyway."

"Not to worry. I ordered the same thing for both of us," he says as the waiter places two steaming plates in front of us. "This is my favorite dish."

I didn't even realize how hungry I was until I smelled the attractive entrée.

"All of this for me?" I ask in disbelief. Jeremy's the only other guy who's ever treated me to a dinner this fancy but not on the regular. We were more of a pizza and tacos kind of couple, and that's just fine with me.

"Me and my teammate, Jonathan were just talking about that," Keenan says before downing a forkful of his salad.

"About what," I ask, enjoying the fresh grilled salmon, steamed spinach and pasta in front of me. I never knew I'd like hollandaise sauce. I may need some more of this to put on everything.

"Why some black women don't feel they're worthy of an expensive meal," Keenan says between bites. "They're quick to suspect that you want something out of them instead of just enjoying a nice meal with an equally nice guy—no strings attached."

The pride in me wants to crock my neck to one side and question Keenan about his observation. But then again, didn't I just do exactly what he said? Sometimes Keenan's too smart for his own good.

"I didn't say that I didn't think I was worthy," I say, refusing to admit any inherited insecurities to this brotha. "I simply asked why you're doing this when we both know your money could go to better use."

Jeremy's family has plenty of money to spare unlike Keenan and I who work hard for every dime we earn.

"Better than seeing you eat the hell out of that poor fish?" Keenan asks, laughing at my near-empty plate. "What's better than that?"

I can't help but smile at Keenan's rationale. He's such a sweetheart. I don't know if we will ever be more than what we are right now, but I must admit I like where this friendship is headed.

"You know what I mean, Keenan. I don't want you wasting your paychecks on expensive dinners for me. I'm content with a five dollar sandwich and a movie."

"Jayd, let's agree to something right now, if you don't mind," Keenan says, reaching across the table and taking my right hand. "Never question your worth with me or any other man—ever. You are worth more than every entrée on that menu, more than this restaurant itself. You are worthy. So just enjoy the meal and stop questioning my intentions, please."

Damn, I guess he set me straight. The truth is I didn't think I was saying that I wasn't worthy of the dinner, just that he needs to save his money for more important things.

"Jayd, that's your problem," my mom says, adding her two cents. *"I hate to agree with the young playboy but he's right. If you don't think you're worth his paycheck and then some you haven't been paying attention to how a real woman operates."*

"Mom, I'm trying to eat my food."

"Oh, you mean the food you don't think you should be eating in the first place? Jayd, you're never going to catch the guy you deserve by doubting who you truly are. My daughter should know at least that much. Girl, stop this foolishness and order the chocolate soufflé for dessert so it'll be ready by the time you two finish eating. Trust me, you'll thank me later."

As quickly as my mom entered the conversation she's out, probably somewhere enjoying her own expensive night with her girls. Maybe she does have a point. My mom's always been considered a high maintenance woman. She's solid in her self-confidence, feels that she should receive whatever she asks for, and she's willing to do things herself if need be. Her man seems to love her for being a woman who knows what she wants and how to get it.

"Jayd, was your food okay?" Keenan asks. This isn't the first time I've had an episode around him. I know he's probably starting to wonder what's up with my space-out moments.

"Yeah, I'm just tired," I say, only half telling the truth. I have to learn how to keep my mom from intruding into my thoughts at any given moment. There must be some sort of psychic doorbell I can install.

"It is getting late. Let me get you back to your car and follow you home," Keenan says, wiping his mouth clean before paying the check. We both cleaned our plates.

"You don't have to do that, Keenan," I say, stretching out in my seat. These yoga pants were made for a feast like this one. "I can make it back to Inglewood from the coffee house by myself."

Other patrons are enjoying nightcaps and dessert. Maybe next time we can do the same.

"What kind of man would I be if I didn't see my date to the front door?" Keenan rises from the table, takes my hand and walks me toward the exit.

"A regular one?" I laugh at my joke but Keenan shakes his head and opens the car door.

"That's because you've been dealing with these boys running around here ruining our sisters' self-esteem. Some of us are gentlemen, Jayd. And I like to think of myself as one of them. My parents taught me well, don't you think?" Keenan asks, closing my door.

I reach across the driver's seat and unlock his door. "Yes, I'd say they did."

"Trust takes time Jayd, and there's no potion for that."
-Mama
Drama High, volume 4: Frenemies

Chapter 11
HEAT

We're inside my mom's apartment for no more than a second before Keenan picks up where we left off the last time he was here. He turns me around to face him, pulling me into his body by my waist. The metal door locks pressing against my back are only a minor nuisance: Keenan's lips are too soft to allow anything to interrupt our flow.

"Come here," Keenan says, leading me to the couch.

I hope my mom doesn't decide to make a mental drive-by. She wouldn't be very happy with the current circumstances.

"It's late," I say. I know we should stop but I don't want to and neither does he.

"Do you want me to leave?" he asks, kissing my bottom lip, nibbling on my left ear and then moving down to my neck. This brotha knows all of my weaknesses.

"No," I mumble, barely able to answer.

I move Keenan's shirt collar to the side and return the affection. He tastes like sweat and feels like pure muscle—just as I imagined. I unbutton his shirt and feel his smooth chest, noticing a tattoo of a woman's name: I'll ask him about that later. At the moment I like the way he's talking to my neck.

"You smell delicious and taste even better," Keenan says between nibbles.

"So do you." My hands can't stop touching his chiseled abs. Football has been good to this man.

Keenan pulls up for air. "You good, Jayd?"

"I'm great." I could lie here forever. His hands and lips are making my head spin.

"Do you have any condoms?" he asks, bringing me back down to Earth.

"Uhmm, no. Why would I?" My mom probably does in her room but I'm not going there again. It was awkward enough the first time my mom gave me the sex talk, mostly because it was on my birthday and she gave me condoms as a gift. I gave those away months ago because I didn't think I'd ever need them.

"You don't use protection?"

"I will when the time comes," I say, propping myself up on my elbows to look him in the eyes. "I'm a virgin, Keenan."

"Oh," Keenan says, staring back at me like I'm a stranger. "I just assumed you had some experience."

"I'm not completely green," I say, smiling at his concern. "Don't worry, Keenan. I'm a big girl."

Keenan pulls away from me and looks at the wall clock. It's two in the morning and neither one of us looks the least bit tired.

"Are you okay with this, wherever it may lead?" Keenan asks, touching my shoulder with the tip of his finger.

"I'm okay with where it's going at the moment," I say, kissing his hand. "If I'm uncomfortable I'll let you know."

"Okay," Keenan says, lowering himself back on top of me. He kisses my forehead, then my nose and continues moving south sending me into a tailspin.

"Who's that?" Keenan asks.

Someone's knocking at my door. I know it's not my mom and Shawntrese knows better than to come over this late unless it's an emergency. It's way after visiting hours and to early for work.

"I don't know but I'll get rid of whoever it is." I pull down my shirt and straighten out my hair. Maybe it's the neighbor downstairs telling us to quiet down.

"Who is it?" I ask, but I can see Jeremy's golden curls through the peephole.

What the hell is he doing here? He must be high coming over this late. The days of him spending the night are behind us as far as Cameron's concerned. Why did he have to come and bring that shit back into my thoughts when Keenan's doing such a good job of keeping the drama at bay?

"Shit!" I say, pressing my hands against the front door praying this is all a dream.

Keenan's in my spot with his eyes closed, resting for round two I suppose. Why is it that every time we try to be alone someone interrupts us?

"Jayd, I can hear you breathing through the door," Jeremy says. "Please let me in. We need to talk."

"Jeremy, this isn't a good time," I say, checking my clothes. "Why didn't you call first?"

Keenan smiles on the couch, signaling me to come back. He's fearless. I would love to not care about my ex standing outside, but Palos Verdes isn't down the street. I can't send him away without at least hearing him out.

"I'll be right back." I grab my jacket off the coat rack next to the front door and unlock the chain.

"Hey," I say, stepping into the hallway. If Shawntrese is home I know she's listening closely for later conversation.

"Jayd, I don't know what to do about Cameron, especially since my parents are on her side." Jeremy's blue eyes are bloodshot like he hasn't slept in days. He looks completely defeated and sober. I've never seen Jeremy look this torn before. "Can't you help me out the way you did last time?"

Jeremy must be desperate if he's asking me to help him with voodoo. We never talk about my lineage but he knows how I get down and chooses not to believe. Funny how desperate times can make you rethink your faith.

"Jeremy, this isn't my battle to fight," I say, pulling my jacket closed. "I've tried but it's evident that whatever's going on with you and your family's addiction problems goes back through your bloodline for many generations," I say, reading the sadness in his eyes. "It's work you have to do with your ancestors. Mine can only help so much."

Jeremy looks genuinely hurt by my words. I've yet to tell him that our great-grandparents were lovers who were tortured by their forbidden love. Our destinies are definitely linked but I don't know to what end.

"I miss you, Lady J," he says, placing his arms around my shoulders. Jeremy bends down, touches my forehead with his and breathes deeply. The last thing I need is more heat to deal with.

Keenan opens the door interrupting our moment. "Jayd, you good?"

Jeremy looks at Keenan standing in the doorway with his shirt opened and I know I'm busted.

"Jayd, who the hell is this?" Jeremy steps toward my mom's door ready to sock the shit out of my date.

"Jeremy, I can explain," I say, but really I can't.

"You don't have to explain yourself to him," Keenan says, stepping outside. "You're a single woman, right?"

Jeremy looks like he's about to throw a punch he's so pissed. I hope it doesn't come to that because—as torn up about it as I'd be—I'd have to put my money on Keenan.

"*You see, Jayd. This is the type of grown man shit you're not ready to deal with,*" my mom says, screaming into my head. "*They're both territorial and dogs all at the same time.*"

She's right. I'm not ready to deal with this tonight no matter how good Keenan makes me feel. He's already got me sprung and we just started talking. My heart still has Jeremy in it and until that tie is broken, I can't move on.

"Both of you need to leave." I push Keenan out of the way and step back inside of the apartment.

"Jayd, are you serious?" Keenan asks, confused.

"*Maybe his fine-ass has never been turned down before, cocky son of a...*" my mom begins but I don't want her badmouthing Keenan, especially not while I'm staring at him.

"*Mom, please*!" I yell into my mind. "*You're not helping.*" My mom sighs loudly and leaves me to my soap opera.

"Yes, Keenan. I need to get some sleep." And that's the truth.

In a few hours I have to be at church and then help Mama in the spirit room for the rest of the day. I'll be glad when we can prove that Esmeralda's responsible for Pam's death. Maybe then I can have my Sundays back. I haven't done this much churching since I was a baby.

"You heard the lady," Jeremy says, his defined jawbones twitching. I haven't seen him this upset since he found out about Rah kissing me almost a year ago. Funny how time flies when you're dealing with drama.

"You too, Jeremy. Goodnight."

I close the door and cry. Why can't Jeremy and I go back to the days of playing chess and making out until dawn? What happened to us?

"*Nothing,*" my mom says. "*You're growing up, Jayd and tough decisions come with the territory. You'll see.*"

Keenan's probably wishing he'd saved his money. I'm not sure if college girls have the same emotional turmoil as I do but I know he's never dealt with as many issues as I bring to the table. It'll be nice to help Mama later on. The busy work will keep my mind preoccupied. Maybe I'll even find a solution to all of my insanity while helping Mama solve problems for her clients. When it's all said and done we have to keep on moving, even through the pain.

Church was full of excitement and testimony this morning, as usual. The church ladies were disgruntled to see my grandmother and her best friend in attendance for the third Sunday in a row, but too bad. Mama and Netta are important staples in the community and it would do those old ladies some good to recognize, much like Jeremy needs to recognize that he can't have his cake and eat it too. Either he's going to stand up for our love in front of Cameron and deal with the consequences or he's going to cave under her ultimatum. Either way I know I'll be fine—Keenan will make sure of that, if I let him.

With all that's going on at home I can't think about choosing between Keenan and Jeremy. Proving Esmeralda's the wicked wench I know her to be to the police is all that I need to focus on. Daddy announced that the coroner's office finally released Pam's body. They can't say for sure what kind of instrument was used to slice her up but one thing's for certain: whatever it was caused her to bleed out slowly and painfully. The news didn't bring much comfort to Mama, but at least we can plan a proper homegoing for Pam.

Netta and Mama came home and worked on the funeral plans as well as filling their clients' orders. Halloween's right around the corner and it's one of Mama's busiest times of year. I can't blame her clients for desiring more protection around the unholy day. Esmeralda's all the proof I need to believe that there's pure, unadulterated evil in the world.

"Jayd, go give this to your grandfather," Mama says, covering the hot plate with a cloth napkin. "He's been outside working on that damn car since he got home."

I stand in the kitchen doorway frozen in shock. Is Mama really feeding Daddy? I must be dreaming of a happy time long, long ago because this hasn't happened in years. Mama swore she'd never serve Daddy or my uncles again and she's kept her word until today.

"Jayd, did you hear me little girl?" Mama asks. "Take your grandfather his dinner."

"Mama, is everything okay?" I say, reaching for the plate of fried chicken, mashed potatoes, gravy, green beans and hot water cornbread.

This is one of those dinners most husbands would love for their wives to cook for them. Mama throws down almost every night, but Daddy usually has to catch his meals elsewhere after he started taking dishes from the various church ladies who love him so much.

"Girl, stop asking silly questions and go on out there before his food gets cold. Make sure you keep it covered."

In a state of complete disbelief, I place my hand over the napkin covering the full plate and head out the back door. I glance down at Lexi in her customary spot and walk down the back porch steps toward the garage where Daddy's set up shop. When he gets frustrated, banging dents out of cars and making them appear brand new is his stress relief.

"Mama sent this for you," I say, watching Daddy paint the old Cadillac in his possession with all the intensity of Picasso. He's so talented when it comes to fixing up cars. I wish he could fix he and Mama's relationship the same way.

"Really?" Daddy says, as surprised as I am by Mama's sudden change of heart.

Pam's murder hit her pretty hard. Daddy's also acting more sullen these days. Finding a dead body in your driveway will do that to anyone with a heart.

"It's not poisoned is it?" Daddy asks, jokingly. He knows as well as I do that if Mama wanted to kill him he would've been dead a long time ago.

"I doubt it seriously. Who would keep the boys in check if you weren't here?" I say, trying to ease his suspicions.

Daddy looks at the plate then up at me. Too hungry to argue, he removes his goggles and gloves and claims his dinner.

"Is that all Lynn Mae needs me for?" Daddy takes a forkful of potatoes and stuffs it into his mouth.

I don't know how to respond to that. It's hard to imagine Mama and Daddy ever being in love, but it was a fact back in the day. The spirit book talks about their whirlwind courtship in detail thanks to Mama's personal journal notes.

"I don't think that's all Mama needs you for," I say, uncomfortable with the conversation. I don't want to put words in Mama's mouth I might live to regret. "I know she loves you. Otherwise, she wouldn't be here."

Daddy looks up toward the house and his eyes become misty. I've never seen my grandfather cry but I think he's close to dropping a tear.

"Tell your grandmother I said thank you," Daddy says, taking another bite of his food.

I leave Daddy to his thoughts and head back inside. Love is a trip no matter how old you are, I suppose.

"Daddy said thank you," I say to Mama as I step back inside the kitchen.

I stop at the sink, wash my hands and turn around toward the two cast iron skillets on the stove. The dozen hot water cornbread patties frying between the two of them are ready to be removed. "Mama, can I take these out now?"

Mama hasn't moved from the kitchen table where she's chopping onions. At first I think her tears are from the stinging vegetables but now I see it's something deeper.

"Mama, what's wrong?" I turn down the skillets knowing the small breads can't stay inside too much longer.

"Nothing, baby," Mama says, wiping tears on her dress sleeve.

"Was it something I said?" I ask.

Mama walks over to the stove and moves the cornbreads one by one onto a paper plate covered with paper towels.

"Words are so powerful, Jayd. They can evoke feelings and emotions you thought were long gone." Mama takes the last of the breads out of the skillet and turns off the stove. I'll clean up the kitchen before I head back to my moms' place.

"I get that, but why are you crying when all Daddy said was 'Thank you'?"

Mama sits down at the table and puts her feet up on the step stool in front of her. "Sometimes saying 'Thank you' can be more powerful than saying 'I love you' when it's sincere. Remember that, Jayd. Love is active. Love is gratitude and appreciation."

I'll have to remind my friends of this little lesson next time we're together. I've never heard love described as a verb before.

"When we lost your Uncle Donnie," Mama says, continuing the lesson. "Your grandfather and I almost fell completely apart. No parent should ever have to loose a child."

Donnie used to be my favorite uncle until crack cocaine hit him like a freight train just like it did to Pam.

"That was the first time your grandfather cheated on me. He has no one to blame for the state of our marriage but himself."

"Then why stay married?" I ask. It's a question I'm sure she's asked herself on more than one occasion.

"Some things are only for couples to understand, chile. Don't be mistaken for a moment. Your grandfather and I love each other, and love is not an easy path to walk. Ultimately I believe we are all soldiers for God, Jayd. And, in the end God is pure love."

"What about false love?" I ask, thinking about my own triangle—or square if we include Rah in the conversation.

"That is lust, Jayd and we've already had that conversation."

As if on cue Rah's call comes through causing Mama to roll her emerald eyes at the intrusion.

"It's Rah," I say, walking toward the back door.

"I know," Mama says, smiling.

I step out the back door and answer the call even if I don't feel like being bothered with any more of his bull. Lexi looks up at me and returns to her slumber. It must be nice to sleep whenever you want to.

"Hello," I say with as much attitude as I can convey through my cell, which he purchased. I think it's time for an upgrade in more ways than one.

"Hey, girl. How's the ink?"

"It's okay," I say, instinctively touching my shoulder where the scab's peeling off. It's not the prettiest thing at the moment but I know it'll be flyy once it heals.

"We're having a little session at the crib tonight if you want to come through. No Trish or Sandy, I promise."

He sounds sweet enough but I'm serious about leaving Rah and his chick shit behind me for good. With both Jeremy and Keenan also on my mind I refuse to allow yet another distraction to get me off of my game.

"Rah, in all honesty I can't afford the gas to drive over there tonight not to mention tomorrow's a school day, but thanks for the invite."

"Jayd, I'll give you gas money when you get here. Girl, you know I got you. Always." I hear Rah's sincerity but I'm not moved to action. Besides, he's never been able to predict the erratic behavior of the females he deals with.

"Yeah, I know." And that's the problem. Rah's always had my heart in the palm of his hand and it's time for me to get off of this rollercoaster ride. "Maybe next time."

"Why do I feel like you're kicking me to the curb?" Rah says, sounding concerned.

I walk down the steps and look at Daddy back to work on his latest project. My grandparents have a special bond that's theirs and theirs alone. Mama said real love is work but our friendship feels more like torture.

"Rah, I'm so tired of our back and forth that I'm getting on my own damned nerves," I say.

Lexi looks up at me in agreement. She's witnessed more than her fair-share of Rah and Jayd arguments.

"What are you really saying, Jayd? You don't want to know me anymore? You don't want to know Kamal or Rahima, either? That's impossible."

It hurts to think about not being there to see Rahima start kindergarten or Kamal graduate from school, but I need to save myself.

"Why prolong the inevitable? If you're going to break my heart again by marrying Trish of all people just do it now so I can get over it. I've got other shit to do."

"Jayd, wait," Rah says, calmly when I'm anything but. The thought of he and Trish tying the knot makes my stomach turn.

"What is it, Rah?" If I don't get off the phone soon I might give in to his request, as usual.

"You know you blew it, right?" Rah says. I can hear his smile through the phone.

"What the hell are you talking about?" I'm not in the mood for twenty-one questions or his mind games. The dirty kitchen is calling and I need to answer if I plan on getting out of Compton by a decent hour.

"When I called you last night I was at the market in the produce section about to buy you a whole chicken and bring it by. But you didn't call me back, so that was that."

"Are you being serious right now?" I ask, barely remembering his call. "You're such a brat."

"I'm not a brat. I'm demanding," Rah says. His supreme ego used to be attractive but I'm over it. "Get it straight."

"Whatever, Rah. Act your age, not your shoe size," I say, quoting one of my mom's favorite *Prince* songs. "If you want to do something for someone just do it—no strings attached. You can't dangle a carrot in front of my face and expect me to perform for the shit."

"Jayd, you're so unappreciative sometimes, you know that? You told me you were a little short on cash and groceries and shit. I'm just trying to help out," Rah says. "No matter who you or I date on the side, we'll always be together in our own way."

"Help out my ass," I say, pissed at his reasoning. "You can take that bird and stuff it for all I care."

I can honestly say a little piece of me has died every time Rah's hurt me. Each time he's lied to me, cheated on me, or chose another chick over me a piece of my heart has broken off and shattered into thousands of pieces that the best super glue couldn't mend. This time is no different.

"Jayd, don't be like that," Rah pleads. "Come on, girl. At the end of the day we're still friends and I want my girl around."

"I'm sure being around another one your ex-girlfriends will look bad in front of the judge, right?" I ask, almost yelling. "Besides, now that you've got Mickey and Sandy out maybe you can move Trish in and really become one big happy family. It's the perfect set up," I say, my voice raising another octave with every passing minute I'm on the phone with this fool. "Sandy's having Trish's brother's love child, and Trish is going to be your step-baby-mama. Y'all can have little incestuous family reunions and everything," I say as sarcastically as I can. "Rahima won't be confused at all."

"Jayd, it's not even like that," Rah says.

I notice he's not denying the ridiculous plan I've laid out in for him. Who knows what the hell he's feeding Trish about their future? Why would I think she's so different from me, falling for Rah's charm time and time again? Personally, those days are over. I will never again take a dude by his word alone.

"Rah, I could honestly give a shit what it's like," I say, looking toward the backdoor. I don't want my Mama to hear me cussing like a sailor. "All I know is that you can take me completely out of the equation. I hope Rahima's best interest is always at the center of everything you do. Deuces," I say, ending the phone conversation once and for all. I love him but enough's enough. Rah can kiss my ass and then some, and he can also take his chicken and bull with him.

"It's just like black folks to fire your ass at the end of the day."
-Jay
Drama High, volume 5: Lady J

Chapter 12
DEUCES

Jeremy hasn't called me since our run-in Sunday morning and I'm not calling him. I have no idea what to say when the time does come. I was slightly relived when he didn't show up at school today. We can't avoid each other forever nor do I want to. But like Rah, Jeremy has a bad habit of attracting crazy broads and I'm tired of catching the backlash.

I should be at the shop this afternoon but when Mrs. Carmichael called to inform me that our papers were ready I told Mama why I needed to leave early. She didn't sound surprised at all. In fact, she'd already filled a larger container of her special honey and olive oil body butter for me to give to Mrs. Carmichael, as if she knew what was coming. One day I hope to rock my powers like my grandmother does. Until then, I'll continue following her lead.

"You hungry, Jayd?" Chase asks, pointing at the carving board piled high with cold cuts, fresh bread and an array of condiments. They eat well around here at all times making Nigel feel right at home.

"Yeah, I could eat."

Chase begins making me a turkey sandwich on rye with plenty of mustard—he knows me so well.

"People are people so why should it be that you and I should get along so awfully?" I sing along with my iPod at the top of my lungs.

Chase laughs at me and shakes his head before passing me the plate. I'm surprised he's not signing along.

"What the hell are you singing?" Nigel asks, entering the room with more snacks. Barbeque chips are just what this sandwich needs to complete the perfect meal.

"It's old school *Depeche Mode.* Familiar?" I ask, continuing with my massacre of the oldie-but-goodie. *Creed* and *Alanis Morissette* are also on this playlist.

"Hell no I'm not familiar with that shit," Nigel says, sitting on the stool next to me at the kitchen island. I love Chase's house. It's not as big as Jeremy's house but it's just as fabulous with an equally spectacular view of the ocean. "And if it sounds anything like what you're trying to sing I don't want to be."

"They're not that bad," Chase says, grabbing the chips out of Nigel's hand. "My mom keeps the band in rotation."

I don't know why Chase is fronting. We both know I downloaded this song from his iPod.

Nigel looks from me to Chase realizing he's not in LA anymore. I know he misses hanging with Rah. I don't think I'll ever understand why Rah does half the shit he does. He's as much an enigma to me as he was five years ago when we first met. As soon I think I know him he pulls a fast one bringing us right back to the beginning. I guess to some people it's nice to keep the mystery alive, but to me it's just plain exhausting.

"Chase, you can't listen to whoever the hell Jayd's listening to and listen to *Little Wayne*," Nigel says, taking a sip from his drink. "It's against the rules, man."

Chase laughs at Nigel but I can tell he's nervous. I would bust him out telling Nigel it's because of the dude formerly-known-as-Chance that I like alternative music in the first place. Chase will be hearing about this later when we're in private. I'm all for him finding his black self but the white part of him is hella cool, too.

"Anyway, like I was saying before the karaoke show," Nigel says, tossing a bag of chips to Chase. "Me and Rah have to find a new supplier. Lance is tripping and it's affecting our bottom line."

"I can hook you up with a couple of my boys in the O.C. but it's high-grade, top shelf type herb," Chase says, pointing to the liquor cabinet in the adjacent dining room. I could probably pay my college tuition with just a few of the pretty bottles in the glass case. "It takes green to get green, you feel me?"

"We've barely been breaking even the past few weeks," Nigel says, frustrated. He needs to take his stubborn ass back home. "What are we going to do? The weed man don't take credit cards."

"I feel you, man," Chase says between bites. "Look, we can take a meeting with them and see what they're willing to invest in a start up." Chase sounds more like a Wall Street businessman than a teenager hustiln' on the streets. This sandwich is too good for me to give my verbal input but I'm taking mental notes.

"Start up?" Nigel says, tossing his food onto the plate. "Fool, we've been making money since you were in diapers." Nigel stares at Chase who doesn't back down. Nigel cracks first realizing how ridiculous he sounds, especially since we're all the same age.

"My brotha," Chase says, imitating Jesse Jackson. "What I am trying to convey today is that you have been dealing with one type of supplier, and I am going to introduce you to his daddy."

We all bust out in laughter. Chase can be so stupid sometimes.

Chase walks around from the opposite side of the island to stand directly in front of our friend. "Can the church say amen?" Has he been watching my grandfather's sermons on YouTube?

"Chance, what are you doing?" Mrs. Carmichael asks, stepping into the kitchen. She still calls her son by the name she gave him rather than the one his birth mother chose.

"Nothing mom," he says, kissing her on the cheek.

She looks great, wearing a trendy yoga suit and sneakers. Mrs. Carmichael's a living testimony of how getting rid of dead weight can work miracles on a person's entire being.

"Here, Jayd. Hand deliver these to Teresa and make sure you let her know that she has exactly three days to get back to me with her response."

Nigel looks pensive at the mention of his mother's name. He has to miss being home, even if his mom's a lot to handle.

"Thank you, Mrs. Carmichael. I'll drop them off on my way home," I say, wiping my hands clean with a napkin. Mrs. Carmichael hands me the heavy manila envelope three times as thick as the papers Mrs. Esop served Mama. Whatever's in these pages is no joke.

I know Mrs. Carmichael's been busy working on her own divorce. From what Chase has said, not only is she going for half of all of his dad's assets—claimed and unknown—but she also wants half of his law firm, and for he and his secretary to be fired for professional misconduct by getting knocked up on company time. Her legal swag is so fierce that she almost makes me want to become a lawyer.

"No problem. And tell your grandmother I said thank you for the sweet gift," Mrs. Carmichael says, smelling her hands. "Text me after you deliver them."

"Yes, ma'am. I will."

It's going to be interesting seeing Mrs. Esop again after all that's happened. She hasn't been in the best shape since Nigel left home and blames one of my best friend's for it. I don't blame Mrs. Esop for being hurt by a few of my actions even if I had no power to prevent them, but she didn't have to drag Mama and Netta's shop into this mess. I hope she's ready because one thing we Williams' women don't do is back down from a fight.

I park my car in the driveway behind Mrs. Esop's *Jaguar*. Her rose garden looks slightly neglected—I guess she hasn't been in the mood for pruning. I ring the front doorbell twice and wait but no one answers. After several minutes I gently push the screen door open and hear two female voices shouting in the living room.

"Mom, this is Regina. She's a captain in the Navy, and she's my fiancé."

"Fiancé." Mrs. Esop looks like she's about to faint. Her husband had better step behind her and get ready to catch.

It's hard to feel sympathy for Mrs. Esop with all of the unnecessary drama she's caused in my life. She's been on a serious power trip lately and thankfully my grandmother is putting it to an end, even if it's probably only temporary. I have a feeling Mrs. Esop always has her nose in someone else's business.

"Excuse me," I say, entering the foyer. I don't want to overhear any more of their family feud—I think I've heard too much as it is. "I just came to drop these off," I say, holding the envelope out like it's a white flag.

"Jayd, is that you?" Natasia says, walking over to me. "You're all grown up." I hug Nigel's big sister much to Mrs. Esop's displeasure.

"It's good to see you, too, Natasia. How's Spelman?"

"It's great," Natasia says, leading me into the living room. "I want you to meet Regina, my fiancé."

Nigel's known about his sister's girlfriend for over a year. They fell in love during freshman orientation and have been going strong ever since.

"It's nice to meet you, Regina. And I love the hair," I say, admiring her short style. "Congratulations on everything."

"Congratulations?" Mrs. Esop says, snapping at me. "What is it you stopped by for again? You know that Nigel's not here," she says, shooting visual daggers at me like it's my fault her son left home.

"Mrs. Carmichael said to give you these." I hand the thick envelope to Mrs. Esop whose eyes slit in anger.

"Natasia, why don't you show our guest to her room," Mrs. Esop says, gesturing upstairs. "We'll continue this conversation later."

"Our guest is staying in my room, mother." Natasia's always been bold with her swag.

"Fine," Mrs. Esop says, holding her right hand against her chest like she's had the wind knocked out of her. "Jayd, follow me."

We step out of the living room and up the winding staircase into her bedroom.

"Mrs. Esop, I'm sorry I walked in when I did. I rang the doorbell but no one answered."

Mrs. Esop looks out of the window where she has a clear view of downtown Los Angeles. My mom would love to live in a house like this. It amazes me how much the homes are in Lafayette Square when the exclusive neighborhood's only a stone's throw away from the hood.

"Natasia's only doing this to spite me you know," she says, lying across her king-sized bed filled with pillows of various neutral shades. "It's just a test, like when she'd throw tantrums as a toddler. She'll never marry a woman, not even over my dead body."

I hate to break it to Mrs. Esop but Natasia and Regina are serious about their nuptials. They have rings and everything. Regina's family is from New York where they'll have no problem making it legal. They're certainly going to be two of the prettiest—and wealthiest—brides I've ever seen.

Mrs. Esop's not really talking to me; she just needs someone to listen to her vent and I happen to be in the wrong place at the wrong time. "I always wanted a daughter to groom into a proper young lady. I wanted to give her the world. All Natasia ever wanted to do was leave me."

"Uhmm, Mrs. Esop, can you please look over everything and get your response back to Mrs. Carmichael in three days?" I say, pointing at the package. "She highlighted each signature line and even tagged the pages to make it quick and easy."

It's ironic how only a few weeks ago Mrs. Carmichael looked like hell when she found out that her husband's secretary was pregnant with his baby. Now Mrs. Esop's the one looking like a truck of despair ran over her ass in the middle of the night.

"I've lost both my children in less than a year, Jayd. Both of them," Mrs. Esop says, taking the papers and tossing them onto the nightstand beside her without even glancing at them. "You give your children everything from the day they're born until you die and they could care less."

"I wouldn't say that your children don't care," I say, eyeing an escape route. "I think they both appreciate what you and your husband have done for them." It would be rude of me to make a break for the door but

I need to get going. I want to start the week off right by getting as much homework done tonight as possible.

"Oh please, Jayd. They both think I'm a wretched old lady who wants to control everyone and everything for my own benefit when that's the furthest thing from the truth. All I ever wanted was the best for them. Why can't they see that?"

"Why can't you see that you have done exactly that? Your children are blessed to have you as a mom," I say, remembering the few good moments we shared. "You just have to see them for who they really are and not who you want them to be." That last comment must've struck a nerve with Mrs. Esop because I can see her fighting back tears.

"I'll have my attorney look over the documents in the morning and get back to your attorney by Thursday afternoon," she says, crawling into the fetal position while hugging a body pillow. "You can see yourself out."

Shit. I knew I went too far but I had to speak the truth. She needed to hear it and no one else seems to be giving it to her plain and simple.

"Jayd, can I ask you a question?" Mrs. Esop says to my back.

"Sure," I say, turning around at the threshold. I should've walked faster.

"Did you at any moment during the weeks we spent together enjoy your time as a debutante in training?"

I gaze out of Mrs. Esop's balcony double doors into the backyard where she's meticulously planted award-winning roses, tulips and other flowers. Her lush, green lawn is immaculate and the furniture is worthy of being featured in one of *Martha Stewart's* magazines. Being a part of her home made me feel like I was worthy of dreaming this big; that I could one day have a home like this. I look at Mrs. Esop's blank stare in the same direction and realize that's not what she's looking for. She wants to know if she taught me anything about being like her in a way that surpasses my actual enjoyment.

"When you taught me how to fold my napkin just so. For some reason I really liked learning how to crease the fabric perfectly before setting it in my lap. It made me feel like a lady." And it did, although rolling around in her custom *Jaguar* made me feel even better. "I've never really used a cloth napkin for anything, but it changed me so much that I went out and bought my own to use when I'm alone." Mine are from *Target* unlike her custom designed sets but that doesn't matter to me. I love eating with them. "If I never said it before, thank you for the experience. I'm sorry it didn't work out as planned."

Mrs. Esop lifts her head from the silk pillow and slightly smiles. I return the gesture and walk out of the door where the housekeeper's standing with Mrs. Esop's dinner awaiting permission to enter. Mrs. Esop signals for her to set the tray down on the table near the window.

"You can come by Thursday afternoon to pick up the papers, Jayd," she says, pushing back her cream-colored Duvet cover and sitting on the side of her bed. It's a trip how depression can cripple a body as much as any physical illness. I'm used to seeing Mrs. Esop working outside or on her away to one of her charity functions, not like this. I wonder if her children know how much pain she's in. No matter what my mom or grandmother ever did to me I'd never want to see them like this. "And Jayd, please tell my son that I love him."

"Why don't you call and tell him yourself?" I ask.

"Because he won't answer my calls. At least Natasia calls me on Sundays even if she only allows us about a minute to chat, and now I know why."

I never thought I'd be the one sticking up for Mrs. Esop to her only son but I think I need to have a chat with my boy about compassion. I can understand him being unforgiving toward Mickey, but not neglecting his mother and daughter—ever. Granted, Nickey's not his blood child but he said he'd take care of her like his own. As Nickey's godmother I often have to remind her parents of their responsibilities.

"Good bye, Mrs. Esop," I say before heading back downstairs and then home. "I'll relay the message to your son."

"It may not make sense to you why a nigga would want to trip you, but that doesn't mean you shouldn't watch your step."
-Bryan
Drama High, volume 14: So, So Hood

Chapter 13
GOLDEN EYE

Because of my wild dreams about Pam and dogs and whatnot I've lost my ability to get that good, good sleep again. I've been meaning to make an appointment with Dr. Whitmore but the weeks keep flying by. The African Student Union has to make an official bid to nominate a candidate for Homecoming court by tomorrow, and Friday's quickly approaching.

For one reason or another most of the girls in the group are ineligible. We have a few exceptions, myself included, but I'm not running. What we need is someone unsuspecting to snag the crown right up from under Nellie's ass. She needs to be punished and humbled at the same time. Once Nellie's fake friends drop her ass for losing the crown, she'll come crawling back to us. Then, maybe she'll rat Cameron out for being the conniving heffa that she is.

"Jayd, please pass me the scissors," Mama says, setting down a crystal vase filled with water on the nightstand in between our beds.

There was a guy selling flowers off of the freeway exit where I purchased a dozen yellow roses to cheer her up. Mama needed my help with Pam's service arrangements after our work at the shop so I decided to spend the night in Compton. Maybe I'll sleep better knowing Mama's in the bed across from mine just in case Pam's soul decides to make another appearance.

"Here you go," I say. I've been folding programs for the past hour. Netta's son has amazing graphic design skills.

"You look tired, Jayd. Have you been sleeping well?" Mama asks, forcing my eyes to meet hers.

"Not really. I've had a lot on my mind," I say, thinking about Jeremy and Keenan, Rah and his drama as well as my own shit. How will I ever be able to handle college with all of this extra bull to contend with?

"How are your dreams?" Mama asks, here eyes probing for the truth.

"Actually, I keep having this nightmare about a rabies infected pack of dogs chasing us," I say, recalling my most recent vision. "You fall to the ground and I look back and run toward you. The dogs are right on top of you, sniffing at your bare feet. I try to help you up but it's like you're in a trance or something. I look at your eyes and they're glowing like Maman's, and here's the really freaky part: so are the dogs' eyes."

Mama continues cutting the rose stems inadvertently clipping her index finger on a thorn. She stares down at the blood pattern on the cutting board and reads the message.

"Jayd, how long have you been having this dream?" Mama asks, still examining the blood.

"It's been about a week now. Each time it gets more and more intense. Sometimes I wake up screaming it feels so real."

"I see." She takes a deep breath, says a prayer in Creole and kisses her fingers.

Mama's not going to tell me everything she's envisioning and she doesn't have to. I can see the worry written all over her smooth face. That's the last time I buy her flowers. I don't like seeing Mama bleed, even if she has nicked herself from time to time while chopping vegetables. It has always made me uncomfortable.

"Mama, what is it?" I take a tissue from the dresser and hand it my grandmother who looks unfazed by my gesture.

"I wish I knew. It's a warning from the ancestors, Jayd—that much is for sure," Mama says, pressing the napkin against her injured finger. "Make sure you record it exactly as you see it in the spirit book each and every time it comes to you. I don't care if the dream is always identical. Keep writing it down and notate any differences no matter how slight the change may be."

"Mama, what is it? I know the dogs' eyes means something."

Mama looks away from her personal divination, the creases in her forehead from years of worrying prominent.

"Lexi," Mama says, shaking her head from side to side. "I think Esmeralda's going to try and turn Lexi against us."

As if she heard us from her in-house spot under the kitchen table, Lexi appears at the threshold between Mama's room and the hallway. What the hell?

Mama locks onto her loyal canine's eyes who glares back at Mama like she's a stranger. Lexi's mouth drips with foam and she's eager to charge.

"Jayd, be very still," Mama says, staring into Lexi's dazed eyes.

Lexi begins barking loudly at her owner; Mama doesn't budge. I never thought Lexi would be crazy enough to cross the threshold into our bedroom but she looks like she's going to pounce at any moment. All the men are in the garage watching the game. I think screaming would piss Lexi off even more.

"Esmeralda crossed Lexi's thoughts with another dog suffering from rabies. She'll regret playing mind games with my girl," Mama says, her eyes aglow. "Jayd, take the corners of your blanket in both of your hands and be ready to throw it over Lexi's head."

"Say what?" I ask aloud even if I meant to curb the outburst. There are two things I don't mess with when they're angry: dogs and bees.

"Jayd, this is no time to be scared. Lexi's our dog. She won't hurt us and we won't have to hurt her if you do exactly as I say."

Technically, Lexi's Mama's dog but this isn't the time to argue semantics.

Lexi's eyes go from confused to lethal in a matter of seconds. She leaps across the threshold onto Mama's bed and attempts to take a bite out of my grandmother's thigh.

"Lexi, no!" I scream, leaping to my feet. I drape the blanket over Lexi's frantic body, entangling her in the blanket.

"Good job," Mama says, wiping blood from her leg. "It's just a scratch; I should be fine." Mama takes the edges of the rowdy blanket and leads the way outside.

"If Esmeralda had the ability to control Lexi's mind this whole time why is she just now attacking?" I ask, opening the backdoor.

"Because she didn't have Rousseau," Mama says, wrestling with her beloved pet. When Lexi realizes what she did she's going to feel horrible. "He can con any animal by becoming one himself. He must've gotten close to Lexi, allowing Esmeralda the perfect opportunity to slip in but that's okay. We've got something for her ass."

"What are we going to do?" I flick the lights on in the backhouse and let Lexi and Mama inside. The warm, sweet scented place calms us all down.

"You're going to write this incident down in the spirit book, take a protection bath and go to bed," Mama says. "I'll take care of Lexi."

"But Mama," I begin, but she's not hearing it.

"Jayd, when you don't sleep you're spiritually and mentally weak. And if you're weak you can't help anyone, including me. Don't worry about my scratches, child. I'll be fine. I've lost too much good sleep in my life to worrying, Jayd. Do as I say and get some rest. Everything else will work itself out in the morning."

When I awoke this morning Mama and Lexi were nowhere to be found. I have no idea what happened after I went to sleep last night—I don't even remember dreaming. The patchouli oil in my bath water was overwhelming and forced me to relax even if I didn't want to. I'm glad it's Friday but would feel better if I could've laid eyes on Mama to make sure she's okay. Esmeralda's getting too slick with her attacks. Mama hates playing fire with fire but after what I witnessed last night, Mama's hot enough to literally burn Esmeralda's house to the ground with the blink of an eye.

"I'm loving this shit, man," Nigel says, showing off his fancy new watch before the impromptu ASU lunch meeting. We need to nominate and vote for a candidate before lunch is over. "These schools are jocking me like females, but the perks are way better than any chick has ever given me."

I know Nigel's in pain over he and Mickey's final demise but this isn't the way to handle it. He needs to be careful about accepting gifts from the various universities attempting to woo him. If Nigel gets caught he's going to find himself riding the bench permanently no matter how good of a player he is.

"Nigel, don't you think you should reject all this crap? Besides, you know you will not be attending any school in Illinois. It's too damn cold for your Cali-bred self," I say, trying to sweetly tell my friend that he's tripping big time.

"Jayd, please," Nigel says, adjusting his new arm piece. "You're the only person I know who'd look a gift horse in the mouth and slap it. You're too suspicious."

"And you're too infatuated with the bling, Nigel." It is a nice watch but still, this is wrong on so many levels, not to mention it's illegal.

"Let the man enjoy his arm candy, baby," Chase says, making light of the situation. He can do that; his family could by the watch company if they wanted to. Nigel's money doesn't go back that far. His dad was in the NBA and made some solid investments over the years that have sustained his family.

"Don't encourage him, Chase," I say, smacking my boy in the arm. "Nigel's playing *Rolex* roulette with his entire future. Is your football career really worth a nice watch?" I wish I could shake some sense into my boy but he's in no mood to listen.

Having played professional basketball for nearly two decades, Mr. Esop knows better than anyone about being savvy with your talent to make it to the next level. If Nigel's smart, he can do the same thing. God gave him a second chance when the shootout resulting in Tre's death spared his own life. He needs to count his blessings, stop trippin' and go home.

"Nah, it's not," Nigel says, removing the watch from his left wrist and observing it further. "But it's a nice incentive to go to school in the Midwest. Hey, do you think they'll buy me a truck to drive around in all that snow?"

"Yeah, man. Why not?" Chase says.

They're both making light of a very serious situation. I wish Rah were here to talk to his best friend since Nigel's obviously not listening to a word I have to say.

"Nigel, stop playing," I say. "You know you're not a man of the elements."

Hell, none of us are. Me and my crew are true LA brats, spoiled by sunshine and mild temperatures. Sure, we have an earthquake every now and then but it's a small tradeoff when you consider what the majority of our days are like.

"I don't see UCLA trying to keep a brotha iced. All they've done is invite me to socials and games and shit. Where's the real love?"

"That is love, fool or has it been too long since you've experienced a healthy relationship to know the difference?"

Nigel smirks knowing I'm talking about more than the volatile relationship he has with our coaches at South Bay High. When Nigel left Westingle to attend South Bay it was a bittersweet decision made mostly by his father, who wanted him to play for the best team in the region—not the second or third. It was a smart move overall but Nigel misses his old school. Rah keeps him in the loop about everything going on, but it's not the same thing.

"Jayd, do I detect a little haterism?" Chase says, tickling my side and hitting my irksome spot like only my play brother can.

"Chase, are you his manager now?" I ask, smacking him in the arm.

"I'm his boy, Jayd. And because I'm his boy I've got to look out for my boy's best interest, you feel me?"

I think Chase actually believes his own bull.

"Does that include him making all of the wrong decisions?" I say, flicking the watch with my finger. If I could throw it in the trashcan to prove my point I would.

"Jayd, you worry too much, baby. Chill with all that negativity. You're bringing a bad aura into the room." Chase takes the sign-in sheet and passes it to Nigel who's busy setting his watch.

"What time is it in China?" Nigel asks, playing with the fancy gold dials. "This watch has three time zone settings. I want to set them all."

"You're too damned silly for me." I can't help but laugh at Nigel's enthusiasm. Last week he got a pair of the new *Jordan's* before they hit the stores. I guess all of the attention is to be expected with a top athlete like Nigel.

No matter how foul the source, Nigel deserves a little lightness in his life after everything he's been through lately, courtesy of Mickey. Speaking in baby-mama drama, Mickey walks into the classroom with her lunch in hand. I'm glad she showed up to the meeting but not for the attitude she's about to bring.

"I see Christmas came early for someone," Mickey says, eyeing the expensive watch before greeting anyone in the room. Damn, this girl can spot bling faster than Queen Califia. Maybe Nickey's gift of sight as a caul child's rubbed off on her mother.

"How's my daughter?" Nigel asks, signing the sheet and passing it to his estranged baby-mama.

"Nickey's fine," Mickey says, setting the food down on an empty desk. "By the way, I don't think it's a good idea for you to see my daughter anymore. I mean, you don't want to be with her mama so you shouldn't be with her, either," Mickey says, signing the paper and passing it to Chase who's as shocked as the rest of us.

"Mickey, what the hell are you talking about?" Nigel asks. "No matter what happens between you and me Nickey will always be my daughter. Check the birth certificate if you don't remember." My boy's vessels are about to pop. Mickey's playing dirty by using Nickey as a pawn to get back at Nigel when this shit's all her fault.

"Well, that can be easily rectified. We can take a blood test down to the county courthouse and change the name if you want to pay for it." Nigel looks like he wants to go Ike and Etta Mae Turner on Mickey. I've never known him to hit a chick but even the most level-headed brothers can slip up when pushed too far.

There's such a thin line between love and hate and Mickey has crossed it. My girl doesn't know the full extent of Nigel's wrath like I do. When he gets pissed, much like Rah, Nigel sees red. He's fallen in love with Nickey, even giving her his last name when he really didn't have to. There's no limit to what he'll do to protect his daughter, damn a blood test.

"Nickey is my daughter, Mickey. Hell, I'm a better parent then you'll ever be," Nigel says, rising from his desk. Chase stands next to him for support. He'll also intervene if necessary.

"Well, if you want to be the daddy then you'll have to act like it. You can start by giving me that watch on your arm," Mickey says, holding out her hand like Sandy does to Rah. "Nickey needs some new diapers and clothes," The fact that Mickey's now reminding me of my former-best friend-turned-arch enemy is not a good look.

"I'm not giving you shit, Mickey," Nigel says, too calm for my taste. "But I'll happily take Nickey to get whatever she needs." Oh Lord, this isn't good.

"Mickey, stop playing. You know that baby loves her daddy," Chase says, trying to lighten the mood but he's never been in the middle of black folks' custody battles. This is about to get real ugly, real fast if they don't stop this train wreck from happening.

"Like I said, when he wants to act like a daddy I'll let him be one. Until then, I'm a single mama," Mickey says, dipping a French fry in ketchup.

"Let me?" Nigel says. He takes Mickey's lunch from the desk and dumps it in the trash next to Mr. Adewale's desk. "No one let's me do a damned thing."

"What the hell did you do that for?" Mickey screams, making us all jump. "You're going to pay for that."

"I have a feeling I already am," Nigel says, unsympathetically.

Chase looks at me and I shake my head knowing this is only the beginning of the storm to come.

"I don't know what's going on but you two need to take it outside," Mr. Adewale says from the doorway. "We're about to start the meeting."

Nigel respects our only black, male teacher and knows Mr. A is a part of my spiritual family.

Mickey and Nigel glare at each other and do as they are told. I'll catch up with them after the meeting. Hopefully by then they would've calmed down.

"Good afternoon every one," Mr. Adewale says stepping into the room with a plate of spaghetti. "Mrs. Bennett can't make it this afternoon so let's get started with the nominations. Madame president, please call the meeting to order."

I follow protocol and begin the meeting, nominating Maggie for the Homecoming ballot. She and her crew have been consistently supportive of the club even before they were members. Maggie will make a flyy and historic Homecoming Queen, giving the Associated Student Body nominee and all of the other clubs a good race. I'm done playing games with my enemies. It's all about winning from here on out.

Maybe if someone fought over Pam we wouldn't be celebrating her homegoing in two days. This weekend is going to be emotional enough without having to deal with Mickey and Nigel's latest episode. If they'd gotten to know each other better in the beginning instead of acting off of their initial physical attraction, then we wouldn't be in this mess to begin with. I agree that they shouldn't be together—at least not at the moment—but they need to focus on what's best for their daughter. Life's too short to sweat the unavoidable bull.

"Deciding when to hold on and when to let go is the wisest wisdom you'll master along the way."
-Netta
Drama High, volume 14: So, So Hood

Chapter 14
AT LAST

"The gold didn't find itself. And I don't care what your history book says, it wasn't Cortes' ass either," Califia says, putting her mahogany hands into the rocks and sea shells at the ocean's shore. After sifting for a few moments, she lifts up a handful of precious stones. "He couldn't see a ten carat nugget if it dropped on his head from the clear-blue sky. He used me as his seer, much like Esmeralda uses other people and animals' sight for her own benefit. No good can ever come from sight thieving for too long."

"Tell that to Misty and Esmeralda," I say. Even in my dreams they're on my mind.

"Look closer, Jayd. There's always more than meets the eye." Califia's large form bends backwards into the tide and becomes one with the ocean. Her long dreadlocks mesh with the sea foam revealing the whales, sharks and various other sea life present just beneath the liquid surface. Her back cascades over the waves before they both break against the shore where my feet are planted.

"Nothing in this life is ever one-dimensional. You're attempting to beat Esmeralda by thinking like a Williams' woman rather than thinking like your enemy. See with Esmeralda's sight and her weaknesses will be revealed."

Focusing on the deep blue ocean in front of me I get caught up in the nearly invisible seaweed moving toward the water. My first instinct is to scream but I stay silent and let the tide swallow me whole.

"Relax into the vision, Little Jayd. Let your mind's eye see what you cannot."

Califia again slips into the mist, freely moving from one form to the next. One minute she's her young self, the next she's an old lady. Her dreadlocks even morph into tentacles from the octopus we saw a few moments ago.

"Focus on the rhythm of the water, Jayd," my great ancestor says, playing in the water." Can you hear the drumbeat?"

I can and it's putting me into a trance. My mind is focused intently on Esmeralda and her growing army of shape shifters. I can see Pam in front of me as if she were still alive. Instead of being her drug addicted self, I see her as the healthy, gorgeous young woman on the ceremony programs she once was.

"What you see is the true Pam before drugs infected her body. Her soul remains the same. Turn your attention to the living dead, as we call them. Even Misty and Emilio's souls are not completely lost, they're just misplaced. See if you can locate the real them."

Being that my great ancestor hasn't met the unwanted members of my crew I don't know if I'd agree with her. She can see way more than I can so I will try and follow her directions even if it's against my gut feeling.

I gaze into the ocean looking at all the sea creatures, taking in the complexities of them all. It becomes clear to me that I am no longer the only one checking things out. They're also looking at me; I can now see their souls clearly.

"They're sentient beings with their own inner voices and destinies, just like us," I say, amazed by their inner voices. "Esmeralda's mastered the art of speaking to their souls."

"Exactly, Little Jayd," Califia says, her face now one with the water around us. "So, if the animals have souls, and your friends shift into their bodies, then the exchange must be mutual, no?"

"Oh my God, I never thought about it like that," I say, the truth becoming more apparent. "Free the animal, free the soul."

Why didn't I think of that before?

"Because your mind wasn't calm enough to see the truth," Califia says, answering my thought. "Now, go take care of business."

My powerful dream got my morning started off on the right track. Six clients later I finally took some time out to tend to my own hair. I've been sporting the slicked-back wet look for the past couple of days and my crown was in desperate need of a deep conditioning. Because we'll be in all white from head to toe for the ceremony, it wasn't necessary to flat iron and set it. But I didn't want to wait until the last minute to get ready for my school week. Tomorrow is Pam's service and Keenan will be here soon to pick me up for our date.

My mom left me a note on the bathroom mirror reminding me to clean up after my clients and to check the utility bills on the dining room table. I can't even take the silver clips out of my hair without stressing about something. Hopefully spending time with Keenan will help me forget about mi vida loca, at least for the rest of the evening.

My cell phone buzzes loudly on the bathroom counter. Keenan must be calling to tell me his on his way.

"Hello," I say, admiring my wild blown-out hair in the bathroom mirror. I wish I were bold enough to rock the natural style. It feels good.

"Jayd, I'm a little early. I hope that's okay," Keenan says.

I run to the front door and look out of the peephole. There he is in all of his sexiness.

"You've got to be joking," I say, opening the door.

"I love your hair," Keenan says, kissing my left cheek. "Aren't you going to invite me in?"

"Keenan, I'm not ready. I wasn't expecting you for another half-hour, if you can't tell," I say, waving my hand at my cut off jean shorts, white t-shirt and poofy hair.

"You need to learn how to go with the ebb and flow of the universe," Keenan says, his words reminding me of last night's dream.

"Was that supposed to be a clever way of telling me that I need to chill?" I say, smiling at his cute self but not moving. I have a precious window between blow drying and flat ironing before it's a wrap. I'm not comfortable doing my hair around Keenan—not yet.

"It means that change is constant. If you embrace it you'll experience what true freedom's all about," he says, revealing a small picnic basket from behind his back. "Come on, let me show you something."

Keenan takes me by the hand and leads me to the dining room table. I shut the door behind us and look toward the bathroom where my ceramic flat iron's waiting for me to return.

"For the lady," Keenan says, opening the basket and revealing a blanket, plenty of food and dessert. "I told you it's special night."

"Oh, Keenan. I don't know what to say."

"Say you're hungry because I sure am." He takes out the blanket and spreads it across the table.

"Is that Ethiopian food?" I ask, peeking inside the Styrofoam containers. My stomach growls in anticipation of the tasty meal. He sure does know how to make me smile.

"This is nothing," Keenan says, taking place settings out of the sides of the quaint basket. "I can make you the best French toast you've ever tasted in the morning."

I don't need special sight to see that he wants to pick up where we left off last weekend. Part of me does, too but I'm not ready to free up that much.

"As wonderful as your offer is, I have to be up early in the morning to help my grandparents. We're having a going home ceremony for our murdered neighbor, Pam." I feel bad that we've yet to vindicate her untimely death, but something has to be done to honor her life. Mama says it's time to let her soul cross completely over to the ancestor world. Even Daddy agrees that it's time to give Pam and the community some closure. We'll never stop searching for the truth behind her death.

"Would you like for me to come with you?" Keenan asks. He sets the appetizers on the table and makes himself comfortable. I never even thought of inviting him to the ceremony.

"You don't have to do that," I say, dipping a miniature carrot into the hummus. This is some good food. I never knew *Trader Joe's* was like this. I'll have to make it a point to shop there more often.

"I want to. Let me be there for you, Jayd," Keenan says, opening the next dish. "There's so much I don't know about you. I want to learn more if you let me."

Keenan is the sweetest brother. It's time I stopped running from him when it's obvious there's more going on between us than a casual fling.

"I'd like that," I say, allowing Keenan to kiss my lips. "I'd also like to finish my hair before we eat if that's okay."

Keenan pulls away and smiles. "I'm not going anywhere, and neither is the food."

Ready or not, Keenan coming to a neighborhood gathering will introduce him into my circle once and for all.

"Good to hear," I say, taking one more bite before heading to the bathroom. It'll be nice having a new friend to kick it with. I just hope everyone else agrees.

We got an early start this morning, piling Netta's truck full of baskets, white cloths, candles and other necessary items for Pam's day. It's going to a beautiful event. Even the weather's participating. I decided to wear a white sundress but realized my tattoo would show. I can't have that kind of attention on me. Mama doesn't even know about my new ink yet and I don't want her to find out about it today. The only problem is that I don't have a white long-sleeve sweater but Mickey does. She should be here any moment.

"Mickey, why aren't you dressed for the ceremony?" I ask. "Mama requested that all participants where something white to honor Pam's spirit."

"I decided not to go but I wanted to give you these to take," Mickey says, handing me a bouquet of white carnations along with the sweater.

"I'll let Mama know these came from you," I say, taking the flowers and setting them down on the dining room table. "What's up, Mickey?" Something else is obviously on my girl's mind but I don't have much time to catch up with her. Daddy will be back from church any minute to change for the service and Mama and Netta are in the spirit room gathering the last of the materials we'll need at the beach.

"Jayd, I'm going to do the right thing and say that G was with me the night of Pam's murder. I'm telling the police first thing in the morning." Mickey looks like she wants to cry but the gangsta girl won't let her true feelings show. "I know this will mean the end of me and Nigel for good."

"The right thing?" I don't mean to yell in my whites but I can't help it. "How in the hell is doing the wrong thing ever right?"

"Right and wrong are relative in the real world, Jayd. Besides, G's always been there for me and Nickey, even when he didn't have to be," Mickey says, romanticizing the situation. "That's the way Nigel needs to learn how to roll. I can't take his bougie ways anymore. He's so damned judgmental it's sickening."

"Mickey, never mind how you feel for a change. Think about your daughter," I say, attempting to reason with her irrational ass. "You can't lie to the cops. If they find out you could wind up in jail yourself and where will that leave Nickey?" Mickey appears to soften but not for long.

"I can't let G go down for a crime he didn't commit. You don't know him like I do," Mickey says, stating the obvious. "No matter what others may think of him he's been good to me."

"Mickey, do you want to go to jail, too? Seriously Mickey, think about what you're about to do before you do it for a change," I say. "This isn't a joke nor is it the time to prove how ride or die you are for your ex boo."

I look past Mickey and down at my goddaughter who's sound asleep in her stroller at the bottom of the porch steps. Why wouldn't she sleep well when I'm around—Nickey Shantae knows I've got her back even when her mama acts like a damned fool.

"Why the hell shouldn't I have G's back?" Mickey says, defensively. "He had me and Nickey when she was first born and still does, unlike your punk ass friend, Nigel who swore to be there for us no matter what."

"Mickey, I know your upset with Nigel but this is not the way to go."

"In case you haven't noticed, I'm Nickey's Mama, not you," Mickey says. "I make the decisions for her, starting with who will take care of us."

This girl's tripping harder than I thought if she thinks G's a good choice for baby-daddy number three.

"Mickey, you can't be serious," I say, trying not to get too loud. "He's in jail. Granted, he's not guilty of this crime but he did kill Tre while attempting to kill Nigel." I know Mickey doesn't want to hear it again, but let's not forget the facts.

"You know that was an accident," Mickey says, spitting she's so mad. "He didn't mean to kill his own boy, Jayd. And it was Tre who stepped in the line of fire, not the other way around."

"Mickey, do you hear yourself talking? Are you saying that it's your actual baby-daddy's fault for protecting Nigel from your crazy ex-boyfriend? That's some bull, Mickey and you have to know it," I yell, damn the white clothing. This trick must be told. "Not to mention the fact that G wrote you cryptic, sick letters about being the whore of Babylon. A few weeks ago you were asking me to concoct a potion to get him off your ass and now you're anxious to give it back to him. What the hell, Mickey?"

"What the hell is that I'm not going back to my mama's house, Jayd; I can't. G's family has been letting me stay with them. As soon as he's out we're going to find a place together," she says, finally confessing her true intentions. "He said we could live in the same complex as his relatives. That way Nickey will grow up around her cousins."

"What cousins, Mickey? Nickey's aunties and cousin live across the street from me, or have you forgotten about Tre's sisters, Brandy and Lydia?" I ask, pointing to my left. "You can't just switch the baby-daddies any time you feel like it. Nigel Esop is Nickey Shantae Esop's legal father and is invested in her well-being."

Mickey starts to cry and so does Nickey. I walk down the steps and pick up my godbaby.

"And so am I. Why do you think I'm breaking my back trying to make sure we have a place of our own and a man around who'll take care of us? Me being a single mama was never a part of the deal."

"Mickey, you can have all of those things but you have to do it the right way," I say, rocking the baby back to sleep. "What about Nickey? She's already attached to her daddy."

"She'll be attached to whoever I tell her to be attached to. I keep telling you I'm Nickey's mother, not you."

"Well then start acting like it by making wise decisions instead of letting your selfish emotions rule your movements. For real, Mickey. Grow the hell up."

"You know what, Jayd? You're the one who needs to grow the hell up. You've never had sex yet you're running around here telling everyone what to do with their babies and lovers," she says, stepping onto the front porch steps. "You don't know what the hell you're talking about. Shut up with all of that fantasy bull, Jayd, get a man and have a little baby of your own since you want to be somebody's mama so bad. Then you can tell me what to do with my own."

Mickey picks up Nickey's diaper bag and reaches for a sleeping Nickey who's safe and sound in my arms. I hate to give her up but Mickey's right. I'm not Nickey's mama no matter how much I care. Mickey can be such a bitch sometimes. This is when I would normally call Nellie to reason with her girl but I can't even do that because Nellie's on one herself.

"Jayd, ride with your uncle Bryan to the beach. Our truck's full," Netta yells from the backyard.

It's time to go. Why the hell did Mickey have to drop this in my lap today of all days? I'll talk to Nigel as soon as I can before he does something rash in response to Mickey's latest stunt. The rest of the afternoon belongs to Pam.

I step closer to the river's shore, washing my feet in the cool water. Accidentally puncturing my big toe on a buried fishhook in the sand, the blood trickles into the water.

"Damn it," I say under my breath, rubbing the sore toe. I take the hook and line out of the freshwater and rinse my toe.

"Jayd, is that you?" I hear a voice ask. I look into the dark water and see no one.

"Jayd, I'm down here," the voice calls again.

I walk into the water knowing it doesn't go that deep because I've been in this river many times before. Almost to the center, I follow the voice confidently until the sandy bed beneath me drops and I go under.

"Open your eyes!" Queen Califia screams into my head. "Your sight will light the way."

I follow her directions able to see underwater. I'm still afraid and rightfully so: The woman's voice is directly behind me and very familiar.

"Jayd, I knew you'd rescue me, you and your Mama," the red-bellied fish says.

I can tell by the way she's looking at me that it's Pam's spirit. The fish looks frail and confused, much like Pam as I remember her. She smiles sinisterly, her eyes growing vacant and I realize that like Lexi, Pam's taken a turn for the worst. I try to swim away but the Piranha follows growing swifter by the second. I'm not of much of a swimmer and the hungry sea life easily catches up to me and snaps at my bare heals.

"Back up, Jaws!" I scream, kicking the fish as hard as I can but it's no use. The water is her territory, not mine. She's using her home court advantage for all it's worth.

"You should know better than to bite the hand that feeds you," Mama says from above, reaching her hands through the water and saving me. When my grandmother pulls me up, Pam's new host body follows catapulting from the water.

"I need your blood to survive!" Pam screams, attempting to take a bite out of my ass but Mama's not having it.

"I hate to hurt you chile, but you're not yourself anymore. Please forgive me, Lord."

Mama takes a large staff and stares at it with all her might. The staff begins to glow, causing it to become energized with Mama's powers. She raises the stick above her head and lunges it into the water, electrocuting the fish.

"Jayd, are you okay?" my grandmother asks.

"Yes, I think so," I say, checking my limbs to make sure.

"You have to be careful what you cast out into the water and with the bait you use. You're liable to attract the wrong thing," Mama says as Pam's lifeless fish body rises to the top.

The water beneath it begins to bubble as hundreds of tiny fish surround Pam. Esmeralda appears on the other side of the river and casts a net, pulling them all toward her.

"Pam!" I scream, sitting straight up in Daddy's *Cadillac*. The sun is shining brightly through the windshield momentarily blinding me. I must've dozed off on the way to the Marina.

"What's up with you?" Bryan asks, focusing on the funeral procession we're a part of. "You're acting like a crackhead—no disrespect intended."

"Shut up, Bryan," I say as I attempt to get my bearings. "I have proof that Esmeralda's behind this debauchery, but it's not the kind of proof I can take to the cops," I say, only half-awake. My head's spinning causing me to feel a bit drowsy. Maybe there's a coffee vendor on the boardwalk. I need a quick jolt.

"Why are you whispering, Jayd? This ain't *Law and Order*," Bryan says, still joking about my situation.

"Bryan, I'm serious," I say, pinching his arm. "I know how Esmeralda killed Pam and how she's taking over using one follower at a time. All I need is a few fish nets and we've got her." Wait, that didn't sound right. I think I'm confusing my dream with reality, but he doesn't need to know that.

"Why are you telling me this stuff? This is Mama's territory not mine," Bryan says, covering his nose as if to say my breath stinks. My uncle can be such a pest some times.

I need to get a message to Mama without tipping Esmeralda and her brood off, but how? Daddy's entire congregation and a few other neighbors came to see Pam's ashes off, and for the free food afterwards no doubt. We made enough to feed the entire neighborhood twice over not to mention what the church folks will serve at the repast.

"Let's go everyone," Daddy says, helping Mama out of Netta's truck. It's cute to see them ride together, even if I know Mama doesn't like to sit in the middle. We're all parked along the metered parking area in the quiet seaside neighborhood.

There's a perfect opening and rock path leading out onto the water. I look at Mama follow her husband and best friend to join the crowd. Once near the water, the fifty-plus participants gather in a circle and light their candles to join in a silent prayer. I catch Mama's eyes and focus on telling her what I need for her to know. My head becomes cool and without knowing how, my mom's sight takes over but I hesitate before entering Mama's head.

"*Didn't you learn anything from your vision quest last night?*" my mom says into my mind. "*Let your mind go free and focus on your intention. The sight will come; I promise.*"

"*Easy for you to say,*" I think back, staring at my grandmother holding my grandfather's hand. One good thing that's come out of this tragedy is that my grandparent's seem closer than ever before.

"*Jayd, focus. You can tell Mama everything she needs to know without speaking a word. Simply think about it,*" my mom says, checking out and letting me do my thing. Esmeralda and her brood stand on the far side of the large circle. She looks younger with every passing day, a side effect of borrowing people's souls I suppose.

"*Mama, it's Esmeralda. She's using the same potion she used on Mickey after she first had the baby,*" I say. That's when Mama and Netta were on their summer adventure down south. Mickey was acting all kinds of crazy, kind of like the bull she served up a little while ago. "*Esmeralda switched the souls of her followers with the souls of her evil animal farm. If we can somehow get our hands on her creatures we should be able to free her victims.*"

"*At last, a solution,*" Mama thinks back. "*If that's what it takes then that's what we'll have to do.*"

I can tell she's a bit taken aback that I figured out how to use my moms powers at-will, but it feels natural just like it did when they first came to me last year. I didn't know how to handle it then but now it's like riding a bike, and it feels good.

"*It's not as easy as it seems. Esmeralda's already made a connection with her prey through the chosen animals,*" I mentally impart. She has enough animals living on her property that the city should reclassify it as a zoo.

"*I know it's like finding a needle in a haystack but we have to find those pets and win their minds back over to our side,*" Mama says, like she's a pet whisperer.

"*And what if we can't win them back? Esmeralda's already turned Lexi against us once and she's the most loyal dog ever,*" I say, shuddering at the memory. Lexi's still depressed about hurting Mama, poor thing.

"*Then we'll have to take more drastic measures.*" Mama's eyes shine brightly in the candlelight adding to their intense hue. "*We'll deal with Esmeralda later. She won't see us coming and that's just how I want it.*"

By the tone in her mental voice I'd say Mama's ready to go wild on Esmeralda's ass, but in this moment she needs to concentrate her energy on the task at-hand. We return our focus to the ceremony where Daddy's wrapping up the end of his prayer. Mama and Netta will lead us in song before Mama has the last word.

"Sister Pam's spirit is finally free to rest in peace," Mama prays over the golden urn. "May God grant her serenity and mercy on the next leg of her journey."

Daddy releases her ashes into the ocean, which causes trained church members to wail and gangsters to pour out a little liquor. Mama, Netta and I praise Pam's energy as the gray dust spreads across the blue water before disappearing into the waves. We will vindicate her life, even in death.

EPILOGUE

Now that Pam's been laid to rest things should calm down around the neighborhood, which will make it easier for Mama and I to do our jobs. Sometimes the neighborhood watch focuses on the wrong people. We need peace and quiet to catch the criminals on our list and no witnesses if we can help it.

"Do you need a ride home?" Keenan asks as we join the procession away from the water. I still can't believe he came to the service. We barely spoke the entire time but he's proven himself to be a good friend and possible boyfriend material. Jeremy and I have so much to work out I can't even imagine jumping into anything new, but this brotha makes it a tempting idea.

"I might. Let me check with my grandmother to see if she needs me for anything else," I say. Before I can go look for her she walks up to us ready to leave.

"Say goodnight to your friend, Jayd," Mama says, giving Keenan a quick once-over. "I need you to come home with us. We have work to do."

I look at a confused Keenan, shrug my shoulders and say goodnight. I wish I could go with him and enjoy the rest of this beautiful evening but Mama has spoken. One day I might tell him more about my lineage and responsibilities outside of my already full existence, but not to soon. Like with all new friends, I can only reveal bits and pieces of my true self until I feel Keenan can handle the rest.

"I'll call you later," Keenan says, giving me a hug. "Goodnight Pastor and Mrs. James. It was a lovely ceremony."

My grandparents return the cordial parting and lead me toward Daddy's car.

Netta's going to stay at the water for a while longer and pray to her spiritual mother, Yemoja. Bryan's also staying behind with some of his friends while everyone else prepares to head back to Compton. Unlike the people who live here, the beach is reserved for special occasions only.

"When we get back to the house we need to seize Esmeralda's brood and free their diabolical souls," Mama says, locking her seatbelt into place.

Daddy looks at his wife, shakes his head and says nothing. He knows how Mama gets down.

"You make it sound so easy," I say, remembering the last time I had to contend with her house beasts. Her favorite pet—that damned crow—sent me into an early initiation process. Thank goodness the unfortunate incident also helped me manifest my powers sooner than later. Otherwise, I would've been that crow's dinner.

"It will be easy if you utilize your powers as only you can. We should have no problems taking possession of the animals. You sure had your way with me this afternoon."

Mama looks in the rearview mirror and catches my eye as I settle into the spacious backseat. I knew she wasn't cool with that move but she doesn't have to punish me like this.

"Mama, how are we going to find out which animal possesses which person's spirit?" I ask. "We can't just go killing them all." No doubt I'll defend myself if need be, but I don't want to get my hands dirty if I don't have to.

"We are not killing them for the sake of shedding blood, Jayd," Mama says.

Daddy shifts uncomfortably in the driver's seat and attempts to ignore our conversation. I don't blame him. From an outsider looking in this all must sound completely insane. Unfortunately, the real crazy lives next door.

"We're sacrificing Esmeralda's wretched menagerie for the sake of the greater good," Mama continues. "If they don't respond to the calming incense we'll burn and we have to kill them all then so be it."

Damn, Mama's gangster with her shit tonight. She's always on point but this vigilante spirit she's displaying is new to me. I think when Esmeralda went after Lexi Mama decided to speed up the ass-kicking process. This time around, Mama's out for blood.

"I'd sacrifice every animal in that damned house if it means saving one human life," Mama says, affirming my thought. "Besides, that shouldn't be necessary if you use your sight properly, Jayd. You should be able to look into their eyes and hear who's who."

All of the sudden I feel a lot of pressure weighing down on me. What if I can't summon my mother's powers like I did earlier? What if I can't hone in on one mind with all of the other animals in the room?

"What about Esmeralda?" I ask, making my final fear audible. "She's not just going to let us walk in and take over."

"Let me worry about Esmeralda, Jayd," my grandmother says, sounding more like a solider on the front line than a priestess. "You just take care of Misty and Emilio's spiritual counterparts and get out of there untouched."

Daddy puts the car in park in our driveway without turning of the engine. As the pastor, he needs to be at the church for the repast. We each have our spiritual jobs to do.

"Be careful, ladies," Daddy says, automatically unlocking our doors.

Mama reassures Daddy that we know what we're doing and we exit the vehicle. He heads back to do his work and leaves us to ours.

"Let's get this over with," Mama says, taking three incense sticks out of her bag and lighting them with a red lighter. She always has supplies on her just in case.

We enter Esmeralda's gated front porch. Mama waves the smoke around before every step we take insuring that we don't cross any traps. Rousseau and Esmeralda are apparently still out but their pets are well aware of our presence. I summon Califia's vision, thinking especially hard about seeing the unseen. Then I'll lay my mom's eyes on them for the finale.

"Lead me to see the unseen so Mama won't go H.A.M. on the innocent," I say, causing Mama to roll her eyes. It shouldn't matter how I deliver the petition as long as it works.

It takes a moment but I can feel the shine in my eyes as they begin to glow. I gaze through the various cages and boxes spread throughout the front of the small house all the way out into the back yard where Rousseau's dogs are on red-alert. If they could break down the back door they'd be all over my ass.

I close my eyes and think about what I want to know, allowing my mom's cold site to come over me like a brain freeze. When I open my eyes I can clearly see Misty and Emilio's souls trapped inside of two rattlesnakes.

"There they are," I say, pointing at the caged reptiles. "The female is Misty and the male is Emilio."

"Damballah and Aida Wedo," Mama says, catching her breath. "I can't kill them and Esmeralda knows it, that evil wench!"

"Did someone call?" Esmeralda says, sneaking in behind us. Damn, she's good at creeping.

"How could you do this to those children?" Mama asks, damn the breaking and entering charge and imminent fight to the death.

"You gave me no choice, Lynn Mae. Remember that." Esmeralda looks up at the wooden beams lining her ceiling where there are several familiar birds perched at her whim—one in particular stands out more than the others.

"Mama, watch out!" I scream, recognizing the beast from my own ill-fated run in with Esmeralda's favorite pet.

I try to protect Mama but the bird's too fast. The crow dives for Mama and pecks her on the forehead.

Blood to drips into Mama's eyes and distracts her from tearing into her nemesis. Esmeralda disappears just as quickly as she appeared leaving us defeated for the time being.

"Let's go," Mama says, hurrying back outside.

I follow her across the path to our front porch where Mama stops suddenly. I step in front of her to check her out. Mama's eyes look blood-shot and drained. What the hell did Esmeralda do to my grandmother?

"Mama, are you okay?" I ask, lifting her chin. Before my grandmother can answer she passes out. Mama's nails scratch me as I break her fall.

"Mama!" I scream, the tattoo on my arm burning from the contact. "Help me somebody, please!" I call out in a panic. I know some of the neighbor's must be home by now. "My grandmother needs an ambulance."

The Baxters, our neighbors across the street, come over to help and already dialed 911. I continue holding Mama wishing I knew what more to do. All we can do now is wait and pray that Mama's okay.

I have listened to my elders; I have been a good girl. I studied when I was supposed to study, did my chores, and provided for others and myself whenever possible. I have been a responsible, compassionate friend and a good daughter. Now the time has finally come to stop turning the other cheek when it comes to our enemies. I hope Esmeralda's ready for the fight of her life. Whatever hesitation I may have once had for completely demolishing Esmeralda and anyone on her team is over. Fool me once, shame on you. Fool me twice, may God have mercy upon your soul.

Discussion Questions

1. Do you think Mickey has the right to take Nickey away from Nigel? Why or why not?
2. Is Keenan good for Jayd or is Lynn Marie right in her concern that Jayd is playing with fire by dating a college man? Explain your answer.
3. Is Mrs. Esop simply a manipulative shrew or is she just misunderstood?
4. Have you considered which colleges you want to apply to? Make a list and give at least five major influences for your decision-making process.
5. Is Rah being a good father, getting played by Trish, or a little of both? Should Jayd forgive him again and maintain their friendship, or is it time for them to call it quits for good?
6. Nigel's being heavily recruited by colleges and accepting illegal gifts...do you think this is right or should he return them?
7. Have you ever had a friend or relative confide in you about being gay? How did you react?
8. Have you ever been a bully and/or the victim of bullying? Talk about these experiences.
9. In light of Esmeralda's union with Rousseau and her growing powers, should Mama per-

manently eliminate her and her followers? How do you think this should occur?

10. Against popular opinion, Jayd has remained a virgin. Do you think it's time for Jayd to sleep with Keenan or someone else? Why or why not?

Stay tuned for the next book
in the DRAMA HIGH series,
NO MERCY

Recommended Reading

Listed below are a few of my favorite writers. The list is in no particular order and always changing. Please feel free to send me your favorites at **www.DramaHigh.com.**

Octavia E. Butler
Alice Walker
Tina McElroy Ansa
James Baldwin
Maryse Conde
Madison Smart Bell
R.M. Johnson
Napoleon Hill
Jackie Collins
Mary Higgins Clark
J.K. Rowling
Stephen King
Iyanla Vanzant
Rhonda Byrne
Amy Tan
Nathan McCall
Nikki Giovanni
Edwidge Danticat

J. California Cooper
Toni Cade Bambara
Richard Wright
Gloria Naylor
James Patterson
Luisah Teish
Queen Afua
Bri. Maya Tiwari
Hill Harper
Joseph Campbell
Tananarive Due
Anne Rice
L.A. Banks
Francine Pascal
Sandra Cisneros
Danielle Steele
Carolyn Rodgers
Stephanie Rose Bird
Chief FAMA

START YOUR OWN BOOK CLUB

Courtesy of the DRAMA HIGH series

ABOUT THIS GUIDE

The following is intended to help you get the Book Club you've always wanted up and running! Enjoy!

Start Your Own Book Club

A Book Club is not only a great way to make friends, but is also a fun and safe environment for you to express your views and opinions on everything from fashion to teen pregnancy? A Teen Book Club can also become a forum or venue to air grievances and plan remedies for problems.

The People

To start, all you need is yourself and at least one other person. There's no criteria for who this person or persons should be other than a desire to read and a commitment to read and discuss during a certain time frame.

The Rules

Just like in Jayd's life, sometimes even Book Club discussions can be filled with much drama. People tend to disagree with each other, cut each other off when speaking, and take criticism personally. So, there should be some ground rules:

1. Do not attack people for their ideas or opinions.
2. When you disagree with a book club member on a point, disagree respectfully. This means that you do not denigrate another person for their ideas or even their ideas, themselves i.e. no name calling or saying, "That's stupid!" Instead, say, "I can respect your position, however, I feel differently."
3. Back up your opinions with concrete evidence, either from the book in question or life in general.
4. Allow every one a turn to comment.
5. Do not cut a member off when they are speaking. Respectfully, wait your turn.
6. Critique only the idea (and do so responsibly; again, saying simply, "That's stupid!" is not allowed). Do not critique the person.
7. Every member must agree to and abide by the ground rules.

*Feel free to add any other ground rules you think might be necessary.

The Meeting Place

Once you've decided on members, and agreed to the ground rules, you should decide on a place to meet. This could be the local library, the school library, your favorite restaurant, a bookstore, or a member's home. Remember, though, if you decide to hold your sessions at a member's home, the location should rotate to another member's home for the next sessions. It's also polite for guests to bring treats when attending a Book Club meeting at a member's home. If you choose to hold your meetings in a public place, always remember to ask the permission of the librarian or store manager. If you decide to hold your meetings in a local bookstore, ask the manager to post a flyer in the window announcing the Book Club to attract more members if you so desire.

Timing is Everything

Teenagers of today are all much busier than teenagers of the past. You're probably thinking, "Between Chorus Rehearsals, the Drama Club, and oh yeah, my job, when will I ever have time to read another book that doesn't feature Romeo and Juliet!" Well, there's always time, if it's time well-planned and time planned ahead. You and your Book Club can decide to meet as often or as little as is appropriate for your bustling schedules. **Once a month** is a favorite option. **Sleepover Book Club** meetings—if you're open to excluding one gender—is also a favorite option. And in this day of high-tech, savvy teens, **Internet Discussion Groups** are also an appealing option. Just choose what's right for you!

Well, you've got the people, the ground rules, the place, and the time. All you need now is a book!

The Book

Choosing a book is the most fun. STREET SOLDIERS is of course an excellent choice, and since it's a series, you won't soon run out of books to read and discuss. Your Book Club can also have comparative discussions as you compare the first book, THE FIGHT, to the second, SECOND CHANCE, and so on.

But depending on your reading appetite, you may want to veer outside of the DRAMA HIGH series. That's okay. There are plenty of options available.

Don't be afraid to mix it up. Nonfiction is just as good as fiction, and a fun way to learn about from whence we came without the monotony of a history book. Science Fiction and Fantasy can be fun too!

And always, always, research the author. You may find the author has a website where you can post your Book Club's questions or comments. The author may even have an email address available so you can correspond directly. Authors will also sit in on your Book Club, either in person, or on the phone, and this can be a fun way to discuss the book as well!

The Discussion

Every good Book Club discussion starts with questions. **STREET SOLDIERS,** as well as every other book in the **DRAMA HIGH** series comes along with a Reading Group Guide for your convenience, though of course, it's fine to make up your own. Here are some sample questions to get started:

1. What's this book all about anyway?
2. Who are the characters? Do we like them? Do they remind us of real people?
3. Was the story interesting? Were real issues of concern to you examined?
4. Were there details that didn't quite work for you or ring true?
5. Did the author create a believable environment—one that you can visualize?
6. Was the ending satisfying?
7. Would you read another book from this author?

Record Keeper

It's generally a good idea to have someone keep track of the books you read. Often libraries and schools will hold reading drives where you're rewarded for having read a certain number of books in a certain time period. Perhaps, a pizza party awaits!

Get Your Teachers and Parents Involved

Teachers and Parents love it when kids get together and read. So involve your teachers and parents. Your Book Club may read a particular book where it would help to have an adult's perspective as part of the discussion. Teachers may also be able to include what you're doing as a Book Club in the classroom curriculum. That way books you love to read like DRAMA HIGH can find a place in your classroom alongside of the books you don't love to read so much.

CPSIA information can be obtained
at www.ICGtesting.com
Printed in the USA
LVHW011257081118
596144LV00001B/22/P